# DÆMON in Lithuania

# DÆMON in Lithuania

## *by* HENRI GUIGONNAT

TRANSLATED BY BARBARA WRIGHT
ILLUSTRATED BY ERIKA WEIHS

*A New Directions Book*

The epigraph is from *Nightwood* by Djuna Barnes.
Copyright © 1937 by Djuna Barnes. Used by permission.

First published in France as *Démone en Lituanie* in 1973
First published clothbound and as New Directions Paperbook 592 in 1985
Published simultaneously in Canada by Penguin Books Canada Limited

This book is designed by Sylvia Frezzolini
Manufactured in the United States of America

Library of Congress Cataloging in Publication Data
Guigonnat, Henri.   Dæmon in Lithuania.
Translation of: Démone en Lituanie.   I. Title.
PQ2667.U4636D413   1985     843′.914     84-22707
ISBN 0-8112-0930-X
ISBN 0-8112-0939-3 (pbk.)

New Directions Books are published for James Laughlin
by New Directions Publishing Corporation
80 Eighth Avenue, New York 10011

FOR BOB SMITH

God, children know something they can't tell,
they like Red Riding Hood
and the wolf in bed!

DJUNA BARNES
*Nightwood*

*DÆMON*
A kind of spirit which, as the ancients supposed, presided over the actions of mankind, gave them their private counsels, and carefully watched over their most secret intentions. . .

*(Lemprière's Classical Dictionary)*

# Various Introductions

*I* was born within the confines of a country that it would perhaps be better not to name—for even though I mention it in the title and in the course of this narrative, it is by no means certain that it is really Lithuania. It was a region of moors, ponds, and dark, marshy forests, against a background of mountains with eternally snowcapped peaks. The castle in which I first saw the light of day contained no less than some fifty rooms, most of which were neglected and unused. It stood on a hill, and was built in the neo-Gothic style very much in vogue at the beginning of the nineteenth century. The surrounding park was so over-grown that its paths were very quickly hidden under tall grasses and dense thickets. It was impossible to tell the difference between the silver birch, lime, and alder trees of the estate and those of the neighboring woods, and even though a tall iron fence marked the boundaries of our land, it had almost disappeared under the assault of all the climbing plants intent on destroying it. It formed a false vegetal barrier that reconciled a park—which in former days, it was said, had been very well kept—with the wild, luxuriant plant life that insinuated itself between the stakes, merrily overran their pointed—though certainly blunt—spikes, and advanced towards the castle, like a very slow but inexorable tide; green, shining, quasi-liquid. Every so often a group of servants, secateurs in hand, would attack a bush or a few brambles. A task that was purely symbolic, and in a way very muddle-headed.

"What an undertaking!" groaned my grandmother Casimira. . .

*

"What foul weather!"' sighed my grandfather Emeric.

And it must be said that it was always raining. When it wasn't raining it was snowing, and when it wasn't snowing it was blowing a gale. Often, it was snowing, raining, and blowing a gale at the same time, and the thunder, which echoed darkly in the deep mountain chasms, shook the walls—and then we used to shiver in delightful fear. This was the country of long winters. . . They began in October, and ended in April. . . At that moment a pale, tepid sun drew vapors up from the ponds, and the fogs of the winter months were succeeded by the mists of the summer months—when the weather was said to be "fine", though in fact it was much worse. It revived our aches and pains; the furniture and our joints creaked. At a very early age I suffered from rheumatism.

As we could never see anything more than a hundred meters away—(if I spoke above of mountains and snowcapped peaks, it was just to give a fleeting impression of the region, as the horizon was always obscured)—we were all horribly shortsighted. I wore round spectacles, with narrow metal frames, like Schubert. . . I liked my grandmother's jet black, searching eyes, with their dilated pupils, and I liked my grandfather's deep-set, equally dark eyes. I liked mine, too, which I qualified as "imperious and melancholy", and—I make no secret of it—I often used to look at myself in the mirrors, and then slowly move closer to them, staring at my own reflection. At those moments I was in a kind of hynotic trance, and I only came back to life when I bumped my nose on the surface of the glass. My face became blurred in the mist of my own breath. I wiped it off gently, stepped back a little, and contemplated with delight—and some trepidation— two dazzling fixed points: my eyes, my myopic eyes. I allowed myself to believe that the gaze of the near-sighted is the most beautiful gaze that exists—providing they don't mar it by pulling faces (screwing up their eyes, frowning, the better to see what they never will see better). . . "I would much rather mistake almost anybody for almost anything, than present a wrinkled, grimacing face," my grandmother used to say wisely—and her features had remained sweet and serene. So, when anyone turned up unexpectedly, she would come down the great staircase with outstretched arms, vociferating, in French: "Chèr, chèr,

chèr. . ." She could thus mistake neither sex nor person. It was only when she had come face to face with the unknown person (of whichever sex), that she could then call out—really much too loudly, sometimes: "Chère Irice. . .", "Cher Witold. . .", "you haven't changed a bit, either from a distance or from close to. . ." People said she was expansive. And yet she had no great liking for visits—with the exception of those of my beloved Uncle Alexander—but I shall speak of them later. . .

*

The entrance hall was, in a way, the castle's prop room. It was enormous, and very dark, with finely-carved panelling on all sides. The great staircase started there; then, after some fifteen spacious steps and a wide landing, it divided into two branches leading to the bedrooms. It was impossible not to admire the elegant curve of the banisters, and their over-elaborate posts. When the lamps were lit, and oscillating in the treacherous draughts, these posts projected eerie, entangled shadows which resembled tropical creepers or crawling snakes. In this decor, you might have expected to find those horrible trophies, the heads of unfortunate, decapitated stags. . . No, though; hunting was forbidden on our estates. The walls were hung with imposing romantic paintings. They depicted a series of mountain catastrophes: a party of roped climbers falling head over heels down a silver-blue glacier; a nice, neat little village just about to be buried under an avalanche; a foolhardy girl being carried away in a foaming torrent—and you could see her outstretched arm, holding a diaphonous

4

scarf, twisting and turning in the swirling eddies. . .
There was one picture missing, I was told—an erupting volcano. One of my aunts—Georgina, I believe—
had taken it to Messina—it looked more impressive
there. Under the pictures there was an accumulation
of umbrellas, sunshades (but why ever sunshades?),
shawls, and long, dark capes, hanging from pegs
carved in the shape of outstretched hands. When they
moved (the draughts again), they could be quite frightening, and we sometimes found ourselves hurrying
past them, in what has been called the Grey-hooded
Even. . . My grandfather Emeric had invented an ingenious system for our boots. The moment we got
indoors, we took them off. We put them on a sloping
contraption, to the right of the front door, and the
rainwater or the melting snow trickled down into a
narrow gully leading to a trough—which simply had
to be changed. Without this clever construction, we
should have come from the muddy paths into a
cloaca. . . On a long oak table there were two enormous saucer-shaped trays. In the one, our inevitable
pairs of spectacles were all jumbled up—and, in our
impatience, it used to take us some time to find our
own. In the other, the letters were piled up. We received an enormous amount of mail, because we wrote
a lot. There was talk of peasant revolts, of violent
deaths, of storms—but what a pleasure it was, despite
our fascination with tempests and turmoils, to abandon the violence of nature and come back to the castle,
feel the thick carpets under our feet, go up to Grandfather, who was collecting, or Grandmother, who was
reading. . . I never really understood the piles of bi-

5

zarre objects that Grandfather accumulated; it was obvious that I was disturbing him, but he never seemed to resent it. At the very most he would show some slight embarrassment, or hurriedly conceal something—I really don't know why. . . As for Grandmother, she was always delighted to see me; she would say out loud the last sentence she'd just been reading, and, by an extraordinary coincidence, that sentence was invariably either poetic or pessimistic. . . It would remain engraved in my memory. When Grandmother turned towards me, her long silken dresses, the color of dead leaves, would rustle, and that slight swishing sound was like that of the innumerable pages she turned over so passionately. . . She used to abandon half-open books on tables and chests of drawers, and there were faint arrows in the margins, marking the passages she had particularly liked. These were never sentences or aphorisms, but felicitous juxtapositions of words which, even if I didn't really understand them then, were evocative of tenderness, violence, passion, love, nostalgia, sadness, escape, death. I studied them eagerly. Grandmother Casimira, with her slightly hoarse voice, with the poetry she remembered and recited (I believe she wrote some in secret) gave me the marvellous, unique gift of a love of reading.

*

I won't speak of my parents. I lost them when I was very young. At the age of three I was an orphan. . . They perished in an atrocious manner. My mother was on her way to take the waters, accompanied by my father. She was growing impatient on the station platform, where she was surrounded by at least a dozen trunks (she had the reputation of being a great coquette, and—I have to admit—somewhat frivolous.) When the steam locomotive arrived, she slipped, holding a book by Tolstoy in her hand. She had no time to suffer: in a single second she had been crushed to death. There was a hideous coincidence: my father stepped back in horror. Another locomotive arrived— and in his turn he was crushed to death! And I am telling nothing but the gospel truth when I say that my maternal grandfather and grandmother died together in a famous shipwreck; that their own parents succumbed, the ones to a no less famous fire, and the others to a stagecoach accident. . . Dying by pairs has become a tradition in my family. But what I hope with all my heart for Grandfather Emeric and Grandmother Casimira—and as late in life as possible—is a peaceful death. Weeping copiously (I rather enjoy that), I imagine them sitting by a log fire. Grandmother is reading aloud; Grandfather is falling asleep. . . Grandmother breaks off in the very middle of a sentence, her head gradually drops. . . They have gone, without surprise, one of Grandfather's hands resting on one of Grandmother's. . . They look peaceful, yet in spite of everything, watchful. . . Later, I follow their hearses. I am elegantly dressed in black. I don't give a fig for any kind of dignity, I sob uncontrollably. . . But one shouldn't let oneself indulge in such reveries.

*

I haven't yet mentioned my sister Kinga (Cunégonde), perhaps because she plays only a minimal part in my memories of my early childhood. She always wore white dresses, which went rather badly with her very pale complexion. Her long hair was dressed in a multitude of braids which were coiled up on top of her head in such a complicated, absurd fashion that I blamed their weight, and their laborious construction, for the doleful airs she used to adopt. She sighed a great deal, she used to sink down on to the divans, and sometimes even faint. She would interrupt her wearisome embroidery, raising her eyes to the heavens (she was subject to strange mystical states), or let the heavy anglo-saxon novels, which she never finished, drop on to her knees. She often held a delicate batiste handkerchief to her lips, and coughed faintly. In those moments she paraded an ostentatious discretion, and a truly unbearable resignation. I kept a pitiless watch on her, and I can positively state that she never coughed the slightest drop of blood. But she had cultivated the art of languishing gracefully, and no doubt her head had been turned by romantic examples of phthisis, of homecomings from balls where you catch cold in the snow. She would often hum waltz tunes, and then place a hand on her migraine-racked forehead. The waltzes were pretty (Kinga was musical, and had a lovely voice which she was anxious not to force), but her attitudes exasperated me. Later, though, I began to like her more, when everything in the castle changed abruptly, on a certain autumn evening. . .

# *All Saints' Day, and, of Course, Death, Just a Little. . .*

*T*hat autumn, the passing flocks of cranes and wild duck were very numerous, and flew very low. On the evening of All Saints' Day we went to the cemetery, less to honor our dead (considering their ends, they must have consisted of a strange bric-à-brac of bones), than to admire the hundreds of lighted candles on the tombs. This was a custom of our region, which did not turn death into a festival—there is really no particular reason to rejoice at it—but which transformed a normally gloomy place (in which, moreover, I never set foot), into a fascinating, fairylike realm in which innumerable flying sparks flickered, launching imperceptible appeals, some of them fluttering like luminous insects. That night, it wasn't raining. . . Wafted on the wind, the perfume of the tuberoses drifted up to us and made us feel slightly tipsy. We walked under the trelliswork of the tall, swaying crosses, and, where the paths curved, the mausoleums appeared like miniature palaces, illuminated for some mysterious ceremony. In these oscillating shadows and sparks, it was impossible to make out the inscriptions of the ex-votos—often singularly inept—, and the dancing letters created a new, obscure, indecipherable language which for a few hours effaced the: "To my dear Mina, whom I will never forget. . .", the "To our little Youja, taken from us in the bloom of her youth (how blooming? and how youthful?)—so many tears shed. . ." (here an urn had been knocked over, sending a cascade of carved stones over the grave). Adieu, Mina, adieu Youja. . . In this place of sorrow and grief everything took on new life, and our dear retainer Baba Sonine (who took care of me, in my infancy, and brought me up in an extravagant way), with tears in her eyes, artlessly declared that all these flickering lights represented souls searching for one another, searching for us. . . In such a scintillating confusion, I wondered how they would ever be able to find us, and it was without the slightest hesitation that, with a steady hand, I brushed away the sparks that might have burned my clothes, or Grandmother's . . . I gazed in delight at the marble cherubs who, as I passed by, seemed to turn their heads in my direction; at the beautiful, frivolous, artificial, beribboned, sanctimonious wreaths, whose colored beads shone faintly, like slightly tarnished jewels. . .

*

At about ten o'clock, we went home. On a promontory, we turned around one last time, and in the long rectangle of the cemetery, whose boundaries were clearly defined by the surrounding shades of night, brilliant convolutions came and went, inventing a thousand changing patterns amid the gusts of wind and the swirling mists. It was like a silent firework display, reflected in a lake. No Christmas tree, however sparkling, ever seemed to me to be more beautiful. . .

*

After that, we had to pass a cross, on which the clothes of sick or dead children were hung. I was forbidden to touch them. That was the last thing I wanted to do. But I walked more slowly, because I was both saddened and fascinated by the sight of those bits of material, faded and frayed by the rain and wind. They flapped in the darkness like frantic wings, and there was something beseeching, something desperate about the clacking sound of those primitively-embroidered little peasant smocks. I was rather delicate, I caught all sorts of illnesses and had to stay in bed more than once. Inevitably, my fever increased the force of any storm tenfold, and I insisted on my wardrobe being locked, and the shutters being tightly closed: I was afraid my clothes might fly off to the cross—that sinister cross on which somber birds would often perch, rip the materials to shreds with their beaks, and, gripping a few pathetic scraps in their razor-sharp claws, bear these ill omens off to some other place.

*

When I wasn't ill, though, I forgot the cross, or I looked at it from a distance, without too many misgivings. I hadn't been taught to make much of a fuss about death. One day I was running down a hill called "the bare mountain" when I stumbled over a skull. I took it back to the castle, where they cleaned it up. My grandfather showed me how to admire its beautiful architecture, and with great gusto came with me to the place where I had fallen. We found other skulls and some fractured tibias, which we took home with us, not without a certain pride. My grandfather consulted an erudite book and discovered what had happened in the district: a famous battle. He shrugged his shoulders, for war disgusted him. But these discoveries of bones overjoyed him. He polished them and scattered them over the furniture, which upset our visitors and finally began to irritate Grandmother. In the end, he deposited them in his study. Grandfather Emeric had just embarked on a new collection—which I found highly fascinating, for that was how I learned anatomy. For once, he hid nothing from me, and it must be admitted that in a skeleton, even when it's in pieces, there isn't a great deal to hide. Quite the contrary. Nor in a body either, come to that, because a body is a future, very chaste, very spick-and-span skeleton. . .

# The Eclipse, and Where
# I Meet Her. . .

*F*or a change, the day after All Saints' Day was very fine. The clouds cleared in the morning, the sun shone, the humidity of the ponds came up to us—we suffered a little, although we had to admit that the weather was exceptionally mild. Grandmother opened a parasol. . . At the beginning of the afternoon a panic-stricken maid came up to the castle, shouting:

"The eclipse, the eclipse. . ."

We rushed over to the windows, and saw the sun gradually disappearing. Then there was nothing left in the sky but a black disc, haloed with rays. This mysterious—and agonizing—twilight disconcerted the birds, who plummeted into the trees like stones, pursued by that brutal darkness. . . The two horses of an impressive lady who was on her way to visit us—

Countess Hedwig—bolted, and she fell into the river, watched by the terrified, paralyzed peasant women. The phenomenon was short-lived, but we remained in the half-light, with beating hearts, breathing with great difficulty. Then a slim crescent appeared. Slowly, the light returned, and the birds, somewhat distraught, began squawking, and took wing again. . . The two horses calmed down. . . The lady, still holding her parasol in her hand (it must certainly have slowed her fall), emerged dripping from the water and came, like a great drowning woman resuscitated, to ask for some clothes from the castle. We comforted her, amidst indescribable chaos. My sister Kinga was lying panting on a sofa. The servants had barricaded themselves into their rooms and didn't want to come out. Animals were running in all directions, and we had to rescue a screaming Sonine, who had got trapped in the wardrobe where she had taken refuge. By the time everything had quietened down, night was falling. In the corridors, they were still talking of portents, but the extraordinary phenomenon had put me into a kind of trance. I had to do something—so I decided to visit the attic.

*

It was an endless attic, and what little light it had came from its ogival skylights. It was never swept or dusted, and a grey, fleecy snow had settled on the furniture and objects scattered around. Spiders had spun immense webs which swayed like net curtains— they too were grey, or rather a silvery-grey. . . I was holding a candle, in a trembling hand, for I was afraid, but it was an exquisite kind of fear, nothing like the afternoon's anguish, at the time of the eclipse. I advanced very slowly, and the candle flame cast long, hesitant, convoluted shadows which converged on me, trying to get at me. I avoided them, and went farther in. At one moment I jumped—at the sight of my image in a mirror; ill-defined, unknown—and I didn't dare linger too long in front of that blurred "me", which was so little like me that I even began to imagine that a gypsy might have stolen into the attic to spy on me. . . The door, which I had left ajar, slammed violently. I jumped again, but instead of rushing back to it to make sure it wasn't jammed, I penetrated even farther into the frightening—I almost wrote forbidden—domain of the furniture swathed in white dustcovers. Why should these pieces have been protected, rather than others? They must certainly have been more valuable or in better condition. . . What did it matter. To me, they seemed like real ghosts—not the kind that are in chains and utter grotesque groans, no, but rather ghosts of objects that had once lived, and that had one day been buried under a sheet, by some egoistic whim. I had the impression that obscure activities were being plotted under their tight folds, and I was afraid that a corner of a sheet might rise, release an odor, reveal a forgotten prop, a crumpled handkerchief, and, why not, the imprint of a body on the faded velvet. . . But they remained motionless, on their guard; then I was in the middle of them and—I'm quite sure—they were watching me. I was almost hoping for a piece of wood to creak, for a spring suddenly to snap, when I became aware of the swooshing sound of wings. Farther on, to the left,

15

quite some distance from the ghosts, there was an ogival aperture, without windowpanes. It was a beautiful clear night. I caught sight of various skimming movements, and I realized that this place was a rendezvous for night birds—screech owls, tawny owls, nightjars. . . But none of them came into the attic. On the skylight sill was a strange silhouette that might almost have been a statue; it was looking out into the night and seemed to be preventing any intrusion into a place which it had doubtless appropriated to itself. My surprise rooted me to the spot. I wondered what kind of animal it could be (it must be remembered that the half-light, my myopia, and my fear, had so far made it impossible for me to identify it.) I thought for a moment of some sort of timid barn owl, but its fierce solitude and bizarre shape finally disconcerted me. In the end, I could bear it no longer: I gave a discreet cough. The silhouette didn't budge, but I thought I perceived a quiver running all along its body, and I saw—what a surprise!—a swishing movement of its tail. It wasn't a bird! My curiosity was at its height. I forgot all my fears, took a step forward, and said:

"Good evening. . ."

A few seconds passed, which felt like an eternity. Finally a head turned towards me, and I saw two enormous golden eyes staring intently at me. My heart was beating, I didn't notice that the burning candle wax was dripping on to my hand. . . I was dazzled. The moon had come out and it formed a halo around the animal's face, as regular as an aureole. I was concentrating my gaze so intensely, and I had come so close to him, that I could distinguish two pointed, pricked-

16

up ears, a flat muzzle with, in its center, the upside-
down circumflex accent of two delicate rose-pink nostrils, a bright red tongue, and brilliant white, very
sharp teeth (the animal had yawned nonchalantly, not
being in the least bothered by my presence), and finally I saw long, long, quivering mustaches, frosted
over like gossamer by the glacial lunar light. . . It was
a Cat.

"Good evening, good evening," I repeated very
politely.

The Cat said nothing. He scrutinized me, and then,
with total insouciance, casually licked a paw. I was
beginning to be at a loss to know what attitude to
adopt when, with an enormous leap, he jumped down
on to the floor, raising a cloud of dust. He sneezed
three times, and I was wondering whether I ought to
offer him a polite benediction, when he shook himself
and came towards me, with a sure, imperious step.
When he had reached my legs, he raised his head to
me, not rubbing himself against them, as a friendly
domestic cat would have done, but not adopting a
hostile attitude, either. He seemed to be waiting. I
bent down over him and noticed that his fur was thick
and silky, very regular, puffed out here and there as if
it had been brushed, and combed, and then very carefully waved. I sank my fingers into the soft, warm
hairs, which were speckled with all the shades of
brown of a tortoiseshell. I stroked the animal with
great admiration—and I was surprised by the ampli-
tude and truly royal majesty of his very bushy tail. He
began to emit a peaceful song, that was not, strictly
speaking—and as people usually say—a purr, but a

17

slow murmur, perfectly modulated and measured, like some foreign chant, basically barbarous, or rather, oriental. I instantly decided to dedicate my soul to all the devils (I preferred, in this case, the plural to the singular—less dangerous, I thought), if the Cat, who was now amplifying his voice, answered my question:

"Are you a Balt? A Serbo-Croatian?"

Alas, he didn't answer. He walked away from me, his tail sticking up, in the direction of the attic door, and as, at all events, we couldn't spend the night in this place, I eagerly followed him. I couldn't wait to announce our encounter.

\*

They were waiting for me, for dinner, in the tall, imitation medieval-style dining room, and we were welcomed by a universal "Oh!" I had taken the Cat in my arms (he was very heavy), and Grandfather and Grandmother almost ran up to me to admire him. I was so excited that I had great difficulty in expressing myself:

"Upstairs. . . in the attic. . . in a skylight. . . this Cat. . . where did he come from. . . and how. . ." I was panting between every few words.

"But what does it matter?" exclaimed Grand-mother. . . "A miracle. He was brought by the wind. . . It's so simple. . ."

Grandfather, in his turn, had taken him in his arms, and was examining him with an air of smug satisfaction.

"He. . . He. . . Are you all blind?. . . What we have here, under our very eyes, is a She-Cat, of the purest, most beautiful species. . ."

A She-Cat! Living in the country, I knew all about the sex of animals, but my confusion at this sudden discovery had led me to simplify everything, in the silliest way in the world. I was furious with myself for that masculine predominance which meant nothing. Even though of a rather proud nature, I recognized my stupidity, and to excuse my blunder I exclaimed, very loudly, clasping my hands:

"A She-Cat! How marvellous!"

I took her from Grandfather's arms and pressed her to my heart. My sister Kinga, who had participated in our joy from a considerable distance, began to play about with her in an idiotic, clumsy fashion. A claw rewarded her with a terrible gash at the corner of her lips, and she began to bleed copiously. Her eternal batiste handkerchief at last found a use. Kinga seemed outraged; she turned her back and started to sob—she must have forgotten to faint. . . Our Baba Sonine, who always had to stick her nose into everything, leaned her big red face over the She-Cat and started drivelling in Polish. She began by saying: "Panie Kochanku, panie Kochanku"—which means: "My dear sir." This was an irritating gaffe—hadn't there been enough talk about a She-Cat? She was a bit deaf, but she was also fond of the drink, and she went on gibberishing: " Aaa aaa, kotki dwa, Szare bure obydwa. . ." All the while pinching the She-Cat's chin, as people do to a newborn baby that they are determined to turn into an idiot. Was it her alcoholic breath?—she kept a jealous watch over her own private samovar, which contained more French (and stolen) cognac than tea— or was it the never-ending flood of her foolish babble?

At all events, she was treated to a terrible paw-whack which resembled nothing so much as a good slap in the face. Three beautiful claw marks appeared on her chubby cheek; they were perfectly drawn, and a marvellously bright red, and they took—I'm not making this up—two months to heal. Sonine remained open-mouthed, but, paradoxically, she had finally found someone who could make her keep her trap shut. . . Grandfather's face lit up:

"But she's a panther, a tigress, a she-devil. . . What am I saying?—she's a dæmon. . ."

And that was what we called her: Dæmon. . . "Dæmon, Dæmon,"—I kept repeating her name for a long time, I cradled it tenderly within me. Because of the upheavals caused by the eclipse in certain primitive souls, or, more likely, because of a phenomenon which provided a totally justifiable excuse for sloth, the fires had not been lit in the hearths. Despite the beautiful day, the night was very chilly. There were even a few clouds passing overhead, and we heard the familiar sound of raindrops beating feverishly against the windowpanes like the impatient fingers of the gnomes in our legends. But we weren't cold. We formed a circle around Dæmon, who had gracefully stretched out on a cushion (even Kinga, even Sonine had joined us—which was greatly to their credit), and we warmed ourselves at her exceptional beauty, at the fiery gold of the looks she occasionally bestowed on us. It was strange: in the center of her eyes there was a compact circle of an intense black, which reminded me of the sun during the eclipse—and I wondered whether there was not some strange relationship between the events of the afternoon and the apparition of Dæmon. . . We sat up for a long time.

Towards midnight, I went up to bed. Dæmon followed me into my room. She slept on my bed, very soundly. But I slept rather badly. I was watching over her. I loved her.

# Pastorale:
# Dæmon's Triumph

*T*he next morning, it seemed to me that Dæmon had grown. I didn't know how old she was—but no doubt my passion exaggerated her harmonious proportions. Never had we had such an autumn, and Grandfather Emeric declared that it was many years since he had known such sun, such warmth, such balmy air.

"My word," he kept saying, "this Dæmon is the harbinger of fine weather. . ."

And the days slipped by, mild and idyllic. It was as if the marshes had evaporated, and there was no denying it: we no longer suffered from rheumatism. One morning we were even able to see the peak of "the ogre's eye tooth", and we decided to go for an excursion, taking a picnic lunch and our alpenstocks. But then we wondered whether this expedition wouldn't tire Dæmon—her paw-craft might not include mountaineering. So we went to a place near the forests, a wooden hunting lodge where, in days gone by, one of my punctilious uncles had shot his unfaithful wife, before putting an end to his own life. We hung hammocks on the veranda, we scattered cashmir cushions here and there, we rocked in wicker rocking chairs. The gentle breeze caressed us, and Dæmon, who was reclining on a faded, pale blue hammock, began to hum, lying on her back with her four paws limply upraised—and we were able to admire the little grey and pink pads which for her were the equivalent of taut, elastic slippers, and on which she walked with such infinite grace. Yellow leaves were falling, and butterflies were fluttering around Dæmon like autumnal snowflakes. She didn't try to catch any of them, she only barely, at one moment, brought out her claws—and she examined them nonchalantly, the way one looks at one's nails to make sure they are quite clean. I was there, with Sonine and Kinga. Grandmother Casimira came and joined us, reading. There were twigs here and there in her grey hair, and it was powdered with the bronze dust that certain plants exhale when the wind makes them sneeze. Some delicate roots and foliage were sticking to the train of her brown dress—she was bringing the autumn with her. . . Then it was Grandfather's turn to arrive, and he started prancing about, chasing butterflies with a net. There was a new collection in the air, but he couldn't manage to imprison them—and he came and joined us on the veranda, out of breath. I was watch-

24

ing Dæmon. Sonine was doing needlework. Grandmother was still reading. She recited a poem about the
life and death of a little shepherd boy; every stanza
ended with the words: "Not like the noble lords. . .
Not with them!. . ." We all took up the refrain: "Not
like the noble lords. . . Not with them!. . ." We were
very comfortable, facing the intermingled purples and
russets of the trees. It's a pity that at that moment no
one took a photograph—one of those autumnal-
colored sepia photographs—of us, and of those bygone days. I can still see the veranda, and us rocking,
and our simple activities, Dæmon singing under her
breath, the charm of that beautiful day, and in our
thoughts the opposite of certain cries repeated in liter-
ature: "To a nunnery, to a nunnery" (Shakespeare),
"To Moscow, to Moscow" (Chekhov). . . For us, even
for Kinga, I think, it was: "Not to Warsaw, not to
Warsaw"—oh no, especially not to Warsaw. . . Kinga
began to sing some arias from *The Tales of Hoffmann*,
and then *The Erl King* (how I appreciated that last
line: "In his arms, the child lay dead.") She ended
with: "Partir, c'est mourir un peu", and, listening to
this song, I felt that the veranda was slowly sailing off,
like a wooden ship, that on this somewhat worm-eaten
craft we should be safeguarded, and I could almost
envisage the moment when we would pull out our
handkerchiefs and wave goodbye to the forests, the
ponds, the hills, the castle. . . Naturally, Dæmon was
steering us with a sure paw.

*

With all this going on, we had forgotten that that
day was the feast day of a Saint whose name escapes

me. When Kinga stopped singing, we heard some women's voices in chorus: it was the harvesters from the neighboring village who, according to custom, were coming to pay us their respects. They hadn't found us at the castle; a servant had told them where we were. They were wearing wide, multicolored skirts, percale fichus, and holding garlands in which sprigs of oat were intertwined with flowers, which they were supposed to offer us, in exchange for a few kopeks, which Grandfather would give them. What the Saint had to do with all that I really can't imagine. . . The harvest women came towards us gauchely, swaying their hips and pretending to be scared. . . Then something surprising happened. Dæmon, who up till then had seemed to be ignoring them, jumped down from her hammock. She crossed the veranda and came to a halt, sitting very upright on her back paws, right in the middle of the steps. The peasant women jumped, then stopped, and consulted each other in a language that must have been a sort of rustic dialect, which we didn't understand. Finally, the youngest of them—a virgin of great beauty and with slightly slanting eyes, shaded by long, silky lashes—stepped forward. She was not wearing a fichu like her companions, and her long hair, in which oats and flowers were interwoven, rippled in the light breeze. She climbed the three steps, as if she were approaching a temple, stopped for a moment, bowed slightly to the She-Cat, inclining her head in exquisite submission (the delightful child! Her cheeks became pink, and her eyelids quivered imperceptibly); finally, she placed her garland at Dæmon's feet. Her work was more beautiful than that of the others. She had taken great pains to harmonize the brilliant colors of the flowers with the more subdued hues of the sprigs of oat and the bronze foliage. It was easy to guess that she had transformed an obscure tradition—to which she was no doubt quite indifferent—into a charming, skillful game which reflected her whole being, in its grace and its inventive freshness.

"My name is Poldzia", said the adorable child, "and here is my offering."

I was so moved that I thought I saw Dæmon smile. In her turn she inclined her head, and then, with infinite delicacy, she laid a paw on Poldzia's bare, very white arm. Poldzia seemed spellbound. She contemplated Dæmon for a few seconds—and we could no longer see the shadows made by her lashes, only her dilated eyes with their jade-green pupils, which were as transparent as the tiny stones in mountain streams —then, walking backwards, she descended the steps. Dæmon didn't insult her by sniffing at the present. She had a charming idea: with one supple leap she jumped into the garland and, in that flowery, leafy nest, she resumed her initial, dignified, sovereign position. The butterflies started fluttering more than ever, and turned into subjugated insects, soaring over her head like flying petals. . . She remained in that position while we each received a garland. Grandfather Emeric distributed his kopeks very generously. I rather believe he was particularly generous to Poldzia, who giggled when he tickled her a little, and nimbly tucked the coins into her low-cut bodice. Naturally, Sonine couldn't forbear to frown, (she was of a jealous nature), but for once she didn't criticize her garland, and Kinga, following her lead, didn't declare that hers was either too heavy or too cumbersome. Decidely, Dæmon was dispensing her blessings to one and all.

We kept repeating: "Thank you, thank you. . .", and many other polite remarks. The harvest women dropped clumsy curtseys—all except Poldzia. They went off into the waning afternoon, and they were caressed by the amber gleams of the autumnal twilight. Before disappearing into the wood, Poldzia turned back. She waved her hand merrily—not to us, I think, but to Dæmon, who was still impassive. Nevertheless, we all waved back, calling out: "Goodbye." Poldzia's shadow lengthened on the meadow. Soon, it disappeared. . .

"The shadows lengthen as the evening falls," my Grandmother recited. It was time to go home.

We turned towards Dæmon. I had the impression that she had grown again—and her tail extended quite some distance over the outer edge of the garland. We exchanged glances without saying a word, but at that moment I think we were all beginning to marvel a little. . . We walked around the garland, and down the steps. Should we call Dæmon, or leave her there? It was certain that she would find her way back to the castle without danger.

In the light of the setting sun, she was looking at the hills behind which it was sinking. Her eyes reflected the light of the evening star, which suddenly vanished. We began to hurry, already overtaken by the first shades of night. . . "Oh, please let Dæmon come, please let Dæmon come," I kept saying to myself, feverishly.

And yet I knew she was still there, on the veranda steps, in her flowery enclosure. She was awaiting the things of the night, dreaming of them, no doubt. But what could she possibly have been dreaming of when I discovered her, turned towards the shadows like that, on the sill of the ogival skylight, in the immense attic, close to those white ghosts? What of? what of? I knew I would never have an answer. And really, it's better that way, I suppose—but it's sad, too. . .

# My Sister Kinga's Leeches

*A*fter Dæmon's triumph, the weather once again became gloomy. . . One afternoon I was in the salon, daydreaming, with a rather grouchy Dæmon for company, when I saw my sister Kinga, who was usually somewhat lackluster, walking up and down in a state of great agitation. She came and went in front of us like a tragedienne in one of her great moments. This exasperated Dæmon, and she began to claw the priceless upholstery of the sofa on which she was taking her ease. I considered the material even more precious when thus devastated, because it revealed its gold and silver threads and resembled the ancient fabrics in certain Orthodox churches—but I realized that even so it would one day have to be sewn up again, otherwise we should soon be sitting on stuffing. This was just a thought like any other, absentminded, indifferent, the sort of thought you get on rainy days.

"I'm in such pain! I'm in such pain!" Kinga was moaning.

This was her usual style, and I was expecting a long list of lamentations about the fashionable nervous complaints or about pulmonary tuberculosis, which in those days was treated by blood-letting or sea voyages. . . Kinga's voice rose:

"I'm in such pain that I think I'm going to smash my head against a wall, or throw myself down from the top of a tower."

This frenzy enchanted me. I didn't believe Kinga would put an end to her days (and in any case, I didn't want her to), but an attempted suicide would in all probability liven up the morose atmosphere—and it might even interest Dæmon. Suddenly, Kinga raised her hands to her temples:

"It's too much! I can't bear it any longer! Ooh-ooh-ooh-ooh-ooh. . ." She gave vent to a prolonged ululation, like an owl hooting. Then her cry stopped abruptly, and, turning towards us, she said, in very distinct tones which I didn't know she was capable of:

"Listen," (she was addressing both Dæmon and me), "I'm going to my room to try to do something about this. Come up in half an hour, and you can help me. . . Whatever you do, don't forget."

She went out, banging the door, and Dæmon and I looked at each other, both privately convinced that Kinga had gone mad. But, well, she had invited us— that was nice of her. I thought she was changing a lot.

*

I had hardly ever entered my sister Kinga's bedroom. She was in the habit of double or triple or quadruple locking her door, of mysteriously murmuring: "I'm busy," and I had given up going to visit her. When I knocked at her door, it was Sonine who answered:

"Come in quickly, and shut the door behind you. . ."

We went in, Dæmon leading. Sonine shot the bolt, which squeaked. The shutters were closed, but the candelabra projected their light on to the pictures of saints and virgin-martyrs with their gazes upturned. The whole room was in indescribable disorder. The armchairs were covered with long, tasselled scarves, with shawls edged with silk fringes; the console tables and chests of drawers were piled high with flasks, gloves, letters, painted fans, bunches of dried flowers mummified under globes, and finally the eternal batiste handkerchiefs. We sat down facing the bed, whose heavy damask curtains were drawn. Sonine was bustling about, with an enormous, dark, outlandish jar in her hands. She was wearing her inevitable wide crinoline skirts and, despite her corpulence, she glided over the rugs like an agile, imposing skater, whose whirling dress had been inflated by the wind. Every so often she stuck her head through the curtains and whispered: "There, is that all right? . . ." "A little higher? . . ." "Should I add some? . . ." We could only barely hear Kinga's plaintive murmurs. Time passed. Somewhere in the castle a clock struck five. Night must have been falling; I could sense it behind the shutters. . . We were growing impatient, and I could feel Dæmon quivering against my body. I was fidgeting, I couldn't keep my legs still, but I finally saw Sonine's enormous face suddenly emerge from between two hangings, like a mask in an Italian comedy which is about to announce the start of the performance.

"It's all ready," she said.

That was a magic moment. She pulled the curtains on the left, and on the right, but this didn't count, as they still didn't reveal anything. Her movements were slow and ceremonious, and added dramatic tension to the pleasure of the discovery. Sitting there in front of those curtains, I imagined I could see them quivering, as they do in the theater when, in that moment of suspense, the lights dim, and the still-hidden stage absorbs every sound, and imposes an intense, tremulous silence. In my heart I could hear the three knocks that precede the rise of the curtain—more than three, perhaps. . . Sonine finally made up her mind. She pulled a cord: the draperies parted, and revealed a shattering sight. Kinga was lying on a white counterpane, her bust elevated by a multitude of equally white pillows. She was wearing a long, embroidered, quasi-transparent nightgown. Her feet were together, her hands clasped. She was completely motionless, her eyes were closed, and you might well have imagined that she was a maiden married to death. . . A multitude of black, glutinous creatures were swarming over her temples. They were leeches, greedily drinking Kinga's blood, and under their constant suction her face was becoming emaciated, her cheeks hollow, and an imperceptible, resigned smile hovered over her pale lips. All the saints and martyrs surrounding her in the oval frames became absurd and pretentious in the midst of their torments. My sister Kinga, and she

33

alone, represented the true Saint, Virgin, and Martyr, and she moaned:

"I am suffering, but I love my suffering. These hideous creatures may suck my blood. . . May suck my entire being. . . I shall vanish, become no more than a shade, a specter, a ghost wandering through the corridors. . ."

She was intoning in a halting voice, and her words were like the last words of the dying, when a meandering delirium precedes death. Tears came to my eyes:

"Kinga, don't leave us," I implored.

I rushed over to her bedside. Dæmon leaped on to the bed. Sonine began to sob:

"Kinga, my child, my darling, my love, stay with us, I beseech you." She dropped the jar, which broke: she uttered a loud cry, and began to bang her forehead against the wall. . . Whereupon Kinga raised a translucid, blue-veined hand:

"Calm down, all of you," she murmured. . . "I need peace, in my suffering. . . You must watch over me, calm me, contemplate me. . . Later, perhaps, if God so wills, I shall feel better. . ."

Dæmon and I looked at each other. On her poor temples the avid leeches were grouped in what looked like little clumps of short, black, viscous, slavering snakes. I had already seen the Gorgons—those fearsome mythological creatures whose hair was entwined with gesticulating serpents. One of them, moreover, was hanging over Grandfather's desk. . . Actually, Kinga had taken on the appearance of a turn-of-the-century Gorgon, evanescent and romantic, not with a great tangle of viperine hair on her head but with coils—or rather ringlets—of wriggling snakelets over her temples, which was very much in the style of the coiffures of those days. Unhappy Kinga: little rivulets of blood were trickling down her cheeks—the leeches must have been working with a will. . . But the jar had broken. Sonine didn't know which way to turn—and the replete leeches, who had torn themselves away from Kinga's ravaged flesh, were squirming horribly all over the pillows. Dæmon approached them. I thought she was going to devour them: their blood, or rather Kinga's blood, could only fortify her. . . No, though; she sniffed at them in obvious disgust, drew her sharp claws, went up to one of the foul creatures and dug them into it with fierce determination. There was an infinitesimal explosion, and the blood spurted out like the purple liquid contained in certain poisonous berries. We were dumbfounded, but we couldn't suppress a murmur of approval. Kinga's cheeks flushed, and her head began to nod.

"What's happening?" she asked.

"Dæmon has found the solution," I declared mysteriously.

These words were all she was waiting for to continue her ingenious operation. "Plop!", "Plop!"—we heard. . . Kinga, intrigued—she was obviously better—raised herself on her pillows. She admired Dæmon's expert diligence, then began to laugh loudly. I began to roll around on the bed, laughing, and Sonine, carried away by this improvised celebration, flopped down heavily by my side, bellowing, and flailing her legs. Kinga's bed shook ominously—but held up. . . "Plop!", "Plop!", "Plop!". . . The little detonations continued while Dæmon deftly harpooned the leeches, and the counterpane and Kinga's nightgown, so white just a short while ago, were speckled with dazzling red spots, a most exciting sight. Really, anyone might have thought that we'd cut the throats of ten victims on that bed! We were laughing so much that we soon found we couldn't breathe. Dæmon gave a great sigh: she had exterminated all the leeches, whose flabby, blackish skins were strewn all over the bed, and sticking to the curtains like fragments of glutinous bark. She stretched out at my feet; we dozed for a moment, exhausted with satisfaction. Soon, the dinner bell rang. We got up hurriedly. Kinga put a dress on over her stained nightgown, and we went out into the corridor. Grandmother, who was coming from her room, screamed so loudly when she saw us that Grandfather came rushing up. I told them what had happened. At first they seemed terrified. But my jubilation, Dæmon's evident exhilaration, Sonine's jovial face, and above all Kinga's healthy mien, which was obvious despite her bloody tattoos, reassured them. Moreover, Kinga declared:

"I have never felt so well. My head is no longer in a vise. I'm still weak, yet I'm full of life. And Dæmon, dearest Dæmon, has put an end to the infernal cycle of the leeches. I have been exorcised!" (Alas, later on she replaced the leeches with a thousand medicines that, more than once, nearly poisoned her—but a great step forward had already been accomplished.) We washed carefully, still roaring with laughter, then we went into the dining room.

*

Kinga drank a lot. (No need to talk about Sonine, who was giggling into her napkin, mumbling:

36

"Blood. . . blood. . .", as if it was the most comical word in the world.) When Kinga left the table she was staggering a little, and humming a song by César Franck. Then she started whirling around, all by herself, stretching her arms up towards the ceiling. Dæmon gambolled around her, thrusting her paws out in front of her very prettily, as if she were trying to catch invisible insects. It was a free, crazy dance. Suddenly, Kinga came to a halt.

"Lord," she said, "I'm quite giddy. My head's spinning. . ."

Dæmon went up to her feet and gyrated around them. There was no longer any doubt: as she was executing these vivacious rotatory movements, I realized that her head reached her tail. . . and that Kinga, still swaying, was encircled by Dæmon's body. . . I found this disconcerting. Dæmon had been in the center of a garland of flowers, at the time of the harvest women's visit, but now Kinga was in the center of a circlet of luxuriant hairs, created by Dæmon! She soon unwound herself—Kinga didn't deserve so much. . . Nevertheless, I was awestruck:

"Don't you think Dæmon has grown?" I hazarded.

No one answered. I realized that we had all become plunged in perplexing reflections, in enigmatic questions. . . Dæmon was lengthening, not before our very eyes, as people usually say, but by surprise, by chance, by making nonsense of time, and troubling our minds. . . That night as I fell asleep, I wondered whether, one day, a Great She-Cat of Lithuania—or elsewhere—might not reign over this isolated and privileged castle.

# Anxieties and Exigencies

*A*t the end of another week, Dæmon had attained the volume of a good-sized dog. It was a great pity that this wasn't the Carnival season. She could have gone to a ball in a sledge, disguised as a large poodle. We would have curled her long, silky hair, lengthily and lovingly, and hidden her face under a domino. (What a mystery, her gold-spangled eyes, behind the moiré velvet of a Venetian mask, still powdered with fresh snow! . . .) Without the slightest doubt she would have been the queen of the festivities when, at midnight, under the crystal chandeliers, she tore off her mask with an expert flick of a claw! But enough of chimeras. . . We had worries. Servants were leaving us for no apparent reason. Whispered meetings took place in the kitchens. We observed frightened looks, scratched faces. One day I saw a maid rushing headlong down the stairs; she had inadvertently stepped on Dæmon's tail, which had now become a long, gliding train, like those behind the dresses of ladies making a ceremonious entrance, or attending a coronation or a court ball. The She-Cat had chased her, growling. Out of breath, the poor girl had thrown herself down at Dæmon's feet, imploring her pardon, and, much to her credit, Dæmon had calmed down and forgiven her. She adored submission. When she was strolling up and down the corridors we had to step aside, greet her, and show extreme deference. . . We had to open doors for her, bring her cushions, put her near the faïence stoves, inquire after her slightest needs. I found this normal. I had never believed either in God, or in the Devil, or in the King, or in the Pope (as for the Revolution, so far I had no knowledge of it), but I had always been taught to recognize Grace and Beauty, and they alone, in my opinion, justified the curtseys, the fervor of our souls, the fullness of our hearts—and the red carpet treatment. At all events, Dæmon was far from being a despot. She chastised all injustice, and once when our Baba Sonine, who prided herself on her taste in poetry, was warbling some reactionary rubbish of the order of:

> *I demean*
> *The Indigene,*
> *I have a go at*
> *The Croat,*
> *I find fault*
> *With the Balt. . .*

Dæmon bit her savagely on the neck. Sonine was outraged; to put a bold front on it, and hypocritically
conceal her pain, she declared:

"If that's the way it is, it's either her or me. . ."

Grandmother, who was leafing through a book by
Sienkiewicz, I rather think, barely lowered her
lorgnette, and murmured:

"Then, my dear Sonine, you know very well who
will win. . ."

And Sonine said no more. She lowered her eyelids,
which were even redder than ever.

The servants became fewer and fewer, a prey to an
oafish fear that spread through them like a contagious
disease. It was in vain that Grandfather increased their
wages, they vanished at dawn or at dusk, and the
moment came when we were alone in the castle. Then
Grandfather had a brilliant idea. He went off one
morning on his horse, and, riding along rutted tracks
through a violent storm, he came to some remote
villages on the other side of the hills. He recruited
adolescent boys and very young girls. Their families,
who were extremely poor, were only too glad to be rid
of them, and the appeal of adventure, of an unknown
castle (and also of Grandfather's generous bounty),
induced all these delightful young people to come to
us. They arrived in a ramshackle old cart like a merry
band of gypsies, dressed in rainbow-colored clothes,
banging tambourines and singing tzigane songs. . .
When they saw Dæmon they uttered spontaneous cries
of admiration. She gave them a warm welcome. The
cantankerous conspiracies gave place to pursuits,
cries, games. . . The girls burst out laughing when

Dæmon insinuated herself under their frilly petticoats, or jumped up on to their firm, opulent breasts,
or licked their necks affectionately. The boys opened
their wide, light-colored tunics and cradled Dæmon
against their naked torsos. They rolled over on the
floor with her, they hugged her, they adorned her with
flowers, with tinkling paste jewelry. . . Dæmon
played with their earrings, climbed on their backs, bit
them mischievously in the nape of the neck. Occasionally, I have to confess, I suffererd a pang of jealousy,
but I forbade myself this perverse feeling of posses-
sion. After all, Dæmon was still sweet, affectionate,
warm, caressing. She followed me everywhere, she
slept with me, snuggled up close to me—I had no
right to monopolize her love, to keep her shut away
like a medieval lady. Bliss had to reign over the castle,
and it couldn't exist where there was suspicion and
envy. . . We had to acknowledge that the work was
somewhat slapdash and disorganized, but at last there
was activity in the air, whatever its nature, and the
first log fire we had lit was dancing gaily in the
hearth—naturally Dæmon was lounging in front of it,
lying on a long, brocade-covered bolster (she certainly
needed that; a cushion would no longer have sufficed),
and we sighed with satisfaction.

Alas, once these domestic worries were over, we had
further cause for concern of a far more dramatic nature. One afternoon we were having tea, and endlessly
stirring our spoons round and round in our cups,
looking out of the windows at the rain which never
stopped falling. Suddenly, we saw Dæmon squat
down and start pissing (there is no other word for so

simple a function, and I strongly object to using the word "urinate", horribly medical, or the expression "wee-wee", totally inane). . . She was usually extremely clean—we imagined that something had distracted her (the weather often made her thoughtful and absentminded) and she had forgotten herself. But she went on and on, and the liquid, which was extremely pungent, I have to admit, went on flowing indefinitely. Dæmon still seemed to be remote, but behind her there was a veritable pond. My immediate—but stupid—thought was that the leeches were taking their revenge. But I was in the grip of a terrible anguish: even a horse, a cow, an elephant—and I don't know what else—wouldn't have relieved itself with such abundance and violent excess. We really could hear the gush of a mountain stream, one of those that turn into a cascade when the snows melt and come crashing down on to the rocks and boulders. . . But this wasn't the moment for such bucolic joys. Naturally, I attributed this unexpected torrent, and Dæmon's total indifference—her apathy, as I saw it— to a dreadful illness that would leave her completely drained. We all sprang up at the same moment. Once again, it was Grandfather Emeric who took matters in hand.

"I'm going to fetch the veterinary surgeon this very minute," he said in decisive tones.

He went out at a run. We mopped up the little lake, and the whole castle, in a state of great agitation and in full force, crowded around Dæmon who was still aloof, barely looking at us. The handsome young man-servants, the attractive young maidservants, Grandmother Casimira, Sonine, Kinga and I, all stroked her, scratched her neck, held her paws, and we would even have licked up what she had evacuated if that could have cured her. We lived through moments of extreme anxiety. Finally Grandfather, and the veterinary surgeon—a bald man who squinted and who looked like a Tyrolean herb-collector—arrived. The vet, accustomed to great hulking farm animals, asked:

"What kind of an animal have we here, then?"

With one voice, we replied:

"Our She-Cat Dæmon."

He frowned, gave a little cough, scratched his yellowish forehead, which was rather like the shell of an egg that hadn't hatched properly. He palpated Dæmon and turned her over on her back. She struggled fiercely and scratched his wrist in every direction, thus producing a regular, and very beautiful, criss-cross pattern. At last he straightened up, without complaining (no doubt the forthcoming kopeks made him forget his pain), and in an authoritative voice, he announced:

"I do not think I am mistaken; it is a serious case of growing pains."

He interrupted himself for a moment, to judge his effect, like an oracle, and then continued:

"She must be given raw meat, very finely ground, and freshly-caught river fish. In my opinion, everything will have righted itself within a week. . ."

There was a wild stampede towards the kitchens. Various dishes were piled up in front of Dæmon. She looked at them in disdain, then, with a single stroke of a furious paw, made a clean sweep of the lot. We stood there aghast, while she stalked out, her tail held high.

*

We had to have dinner, though, after so much excitement. Dæmon came and joined us. . . We watched her out of the corner of our eye, and then we put down on the rugs plateful of exquisite poultry (our new and charming cook, Marietta, prepared the most succulent dishes). Dæmon spurned them. They remained there, pathetically abandoned, like offerings that a fastidious goddess has rejected, expecting something better—but what? We had no appetite. We sighed, crumbled up our bread, played absentmindedly with our knives and forks. Baba drank like a true Polishwoman, and Kinga started snivelling. When the dessert arrived ("Czech straws", a kind of shortcake, cut into thin slivers, fried in butter and sugar, and covered in hot chocolate sauce), a veritable hurricane was unleashed. Dæmon leaped up on to the table, knocked over the candlesticks, the bottles, a few glasses, pounced on Grandfather's plate and avidly lapped up the exquisite delicacy. Then she looked at us all cantankerously, took a sideswipe at the few remaining glasses, ripped up the delicate lace-embroidered tablecloth that had been brought out of our ancestors' wardrobes, and fled, growling in terrifying fashion. Needless to say, we all sat there transfixed, and Grandmother's hair, usually so immaculate, was now sticking out in all directions, as if she had been through a tornado. Sonine, in a stupor, crossed her fingers and held both hands up in the air, twirling them around like ridiculous, superstitious weathercocks. . .

"I do hope she isn't having an epileptic fit," she

couldn't forbear to opine. "In my village, once. . ."

"That's enough," Grandfather interrupted. "Let's go up to bed."

And we went up, despondent, demoralized, our necks and shoulders bowed down under a heavy weight. A violent storm was raging, and in my nightmares I thought Dæmon was breathing new life into the ferocious elements, that she was flying above the gales like a feline witch, and furiously knocking on the castle shutters with the intention of destroying them for evermore—and us with them. . . That night, she didn't sleep with me.

The next day, at lunch, during which an oppressive silence reigned, the same terrible event recurred. We had been chewing at our food without the slightest appetite, when the dessert was brought in: this time it was "Zwetschkenknödel", a sort of turnover; pastry filled with plums, cooked, and served with sugar. Dæmon's violence outdid that of the day before. She didn't jump up on to the table, she grabbed hold of the tablecloth with her teeth and with her multiple claws, as sharp and sparkling as stalactites, and the whole lot came crashing down as if all hell had been let loose. Sonine followed suit, and started rolling around on the carpet. Kinga fled, shrieking. Grandfather, Grandmother and I were besmirched from head to foot with bits of food. Dæmon wasn't the slightest bit perturbed. She began to growl again, even more ferociously than the previous evening, arched her back so high that another cat could easily have passed underneath her, as in a charming ballet (but we were very far removed from such graceful actions), and she finally began to gobble up every remaining scrap of the "Zwetsch-kenknödel" scattered all over the carpet. . .

We were subjected to these atrocious outbursts six times running, and six times at dessert. We were beginning to get thinner. Dæmon was getting fatter, and she was still growing. . . Finally, Grandfather Emeric called us all together one day, in the little salon where Grandmother usually wrote her letters. He adopted a very serious air, and said:

"I have been thinking" (we had all been "thinking", both sadly and bitterly). I have discovered three important facts: in the first place, Dæmon likes desserts. So Marietta must make them for her, and the most delectable ones. Next, after much close observation, it is easy to see that she is a vegetarian. But as she cannot be nourished exclusively on sweetmeats, we shall have to take great pains to see that she has a balanced diet, to make it rich in calories, and above all to eliminate all animal flesh. And finally: her virulence towards us proves that she feels rejected, and maybe even an outcast, when we take our meals. I suggest that she should lunch and dine in our company. . .

I can still see us, surrounding Grandfather, listening to him first attentively and then excitedly. Dusk was falling, and the approaching dinner hour was obviously going to be a crucial moment, a veritable ceremony, which we would remember for a very long time.

*

An extra armchair had been brought up. Several luxurious cushions covered in silk brocade were piled

46

up on it. When the bell rang, I called Dæmon. She came in, showed not the slightest sign of surprise, walked straight up to her place, jumped up nimbly, and settled down comfortably as if nothing had happened. Set out in front of her were a plate and a goblet, the latter filled with fresh water, both made of the finest porcelain with a leafy pattern. We had taken great care with our attire. All the vases were full of flowers hanging down in perfumed cascades. The candle flames danced in Dæmon's eyes like crafty little goblins reflected through the windowpanes. While we were waiting for the dishes to be brought in, she toyed gracefully, charmingly, with the brown-speckled, purple petals of a martagon lily (this genus has become rare in our regions). She was given "Kolduny"—a kind of ravioli from which all trace of mutton had been removed with infinite pains; "Bigos"—cabbage gently simmered for a long time; stuffed eggs; and finally, rolled-up pancakes filled with whipped cream. She obviously had a very hearty appetite, and she wasn't even averse to a few mouthfuls of the French champagne we all adored. Dæmon looked at us benevolently, hummed, licked her chops. At the end of this banquet she opened her mouth; we thought the first signs of her digestion were about to be manifested in a yawn. No, though: she belched loudly. We jumped—certainly not in indignation (after all, this reaction signified the height of bliss), but because we were so surprised by such a cavernous sound. A little tipsy with the champagne, we all belched in chorus, with great spontaneity and a certain harmony. Then Dæmon emitted a brisk, lively sound with her behind. It was not our custom to fart at table, and Grandmother began to fidget a little on her chair. But actually, what's the difference between one sound and another, when they both come from the same body? Dæmon was teaching us flexibility, and we all let ourselves go, especially Sonine, who stank the room out with somewhat excessive insistence (later, we shocked more than one guest, forgetting as we did the false requirements of common courtesy, and if this put a distance between us and those of our visitors who were sticklers for their principles, it only strengthened our own bonds, thanks to this benevolent physiological liberty). I was thinking that this was where it would stop, when Dæmon meowed—an outlandish meow which became more and more high-pitched, like a slightly tipsy soprano vocalizing. When she reached the top note she stopped, and looked at Kinga. They meowed together, and it was like a chorus of mischievous birds chirruping on a tree, perching on higher and higher branches. After a while they were up in the most melodious of clouds. Then Grandmother too had a go. But her voice was less crystalline, it couldn't go so high. She meowed with sweet equipoise, to the air of a *lied*. Sonine bombinated, gutturalized, and choked like a hapless asthmatic cat. Grandfather was perfect. . . His low-pitched, circumspect timbre was less evocative of a song than of an obscure story intended to be told, eyes rolling, around a fireside, to arouse fear. . . But there was a hint of irony in it, and Dæmon seemed interested and amused. In my turn I wanted to try my luck, but my voice was breaking, and I modulated in ghastly fashion from the lowest to the most strident notes. Dæmon displayed the most exquisite courtesy: she gave me—if I can so put it—the "A", and I managed to follow her in a vibrato that sent a long shiver through the crystal glasses, which finally began to jingle like the bells of a far-off sleigh.

. . . I collapsed on to the table. I must have been a little drunk, it was late, and I was overcome by the intense concentration and stupefaction with which I had been following this impromptu concert. I seem to remember, though, that I had a kind of lightning vision: attired in ceremonial dress, we were all on a platform draped with purple velvet. The audience was becoming impatient. Suddenly, a maestro appeared: this was Dæmon, standing up, extending her immense claws, like sharpened conductors' batons. The spectators fell silent. Dæmon stamped an authoritative paw on the carpet. We coughed discreetly, held our breath, waited a few seconds, and then launched into an admirable quintet of meows. In the bedazzled audience, more than one eye misted over. . .

# Our Baba Sonine's Tail

*D*æmon was now as big as a healthy sheep dog. Her glossy tail swept along the floor with sovereign dignity, and, as she grew, we removed her cushions one by one. Soon she was sitting on her chair just like you and me—though I was only a myopic little boy and I still had, I have to admit, a cushion under my behind. . . We had to be light-hearted, nonchalant, lazy. Nothing surprised us, and one single fact will suffice to prove our insouciance at that time. We took great care to see that Dæmon's muzzle never came anywhere near the meat she abhorred; in our domains, as I have already said, hunting and shooting were forbidden and the animals, like the trees, died a natural death. . . But we surreptitiously sent the servants to buy poultry in the nearby markets, and I even believe that my Grandfather Emeric paid shady-looking men to go poaching in properties that didn't belong to us. In short, we more or less closed our eyes to what we didn't want to see, but we hadn't the strength of character to deprive ourselves of what we so enjoyed. Sometimes, though, we felt the twinges of a guilty conscience at the sight of Dæmon and her hothouse vegetables, exquisitely prepared and set out all around her in pretty, tempting colors.

We spent a great deal of time at table, and it was once again during a meal that something happened which I found deeply disturbing. . . First, however, I must make it clear that we were not gluttons. . . Nevertheless, because of the isolation of the region, the dreadful weather, the greyness of the long-drawn-out grey days, we used to seize on the slightest occasion to get together. What could be better than agapes? We had breakfast in a boudoir hung with blue silk tapestries, adjoining Grandmother's bedroom, where we would read our letters and the newspapers—already several days old—and comment on them. As I have already mentioned, we lunched and dined in the imposing gothic dining room. We had tea, according to our fancy and the weather, here or there. . . Sometimes we improvised light repasts, and some nights, after our reading and long, animated conversations, we decided to have a midnight feast. At that rate we might well have become very corpulent, but we were svelte by nature and we also had a horror of obesity, so we mostly tended just to nibble at our food although occasionally, I have to admit, we indulged in great gormandizing frenzies which left us exhausted and comatose. . . Luckily these moments of folly were of short duration.

Sonine was—if that is what you can call it—the heroine of the drama. She wore very full, stiff skirts, which rustled when she moved, and overturned fragile, valuable pieces of furniture. We were always asking her whether her attire didn't hamper her. She got very angry. She declared that she wished to follow the customs of her village, which decreed that every virgin who was not married by the age of twenty must every year add one more petticoat under her dress. It gave me the shivers when I thought about old ladies of ninety who were still maidens. . . People (and especially women) lived to a ripe old age in those parts; how could they move around, poor things, wearing seventy petticoats? How could they dress and undress, and go about their everyday activities? I supposed that they slept and died standing up, supported by their starched petticoats, their arms dangling, their busts drooping, like scarecrows with their clothes whipped up by a high wind. . . Naturally, Sonine, who was of inordinate pride, resented her celibacy. She gave us to understand that men were always saying sweet nothings to her, and she went to great pains to show us how amusing she was, declaring coquettishly that her suitors didn't just pull petals off daisies for her, but lifted, one by one, her white petticoats. Given their weight and the number of times they had been starched, this task seemed to me to be more than fatiguing. But to what extremes may one not be driven by love?

. . . We were at table, then. Suddenly, a violent wind arose, sending whole bundles of brushwood and dead leaves flying against the windows. At one stroke, night had fallen over the castle, like an immense black cloak. Sonine had got up to go and fetch a candelabrum. As she came back, the door abruptly slammed behind her, imprisoning her dress. She looked as if she had been struck by lightning. She dropped the heavy sconce, gave vent to the most ghastly shrieks, as if her throat were being cut, tugged at her skirts with all her might, with the result that they tore from bottom to top with a sinister crackling sound. . . We were struck dumb with amazement! In the jumbled tatters of poor Sonine's petticoats, it wasn't her behind that we saw (I imagined it as white, rounded, and very plump), but a long, black, hairy appendage, with greyish spots here and there, ending in a more luxuriant tuft like a squirrel's plume. It was a tail! Our Baba Sonine had a tail! She poured out a string of horrible imprecations, she gathered together, as best she could, her clothes— or rather, her rags—and fled, cursing the castle, cursing us all. . . The blood was throbbing in my ears. Kinga's mouth remained wide open, her fork halfway up to it. Grandmother's lorgnette shook in her hand. Grandfather mopped his brow. Gathering my wits a little, I noticed that Dæmon had turned her head and was looking suspiciously at her own tail, which was waving from left to right. She must have been irritated at discovering her unusual relationship with our Baba Sonine whom she considered, I think, rather stupid, but her own tail was much more beautiful: more flourishing, more full-blown—you might even say more

glorious. . . Grandfather looked at us one after the other, and for a moment his eyes lingered, insistently, on Dæmon.

"Luckily," he declared, "there were no servants present. Listen to me carefully; WE SAW NOTHING; do you understand?: SAW NOTHING."

With one accord, we acquiesced:

"Naturally, we saw nothing, we saw nothing at all."

But our voices dropped, at the same time as in our imagination Sonine's tail swelled, uncoiled like a sinuous reptile, turned into something thick, bushy, and rough, like horsehair; broadened and lengthened out of all proportion—and we wondered whether we were not still living in the times when witchcraft was rife. Dæmon seemed extremely intrigued, and even somewhat bizarre. . . I believe that a big imaginary tail formed a great bond between us all.

*

Grandfather went and knocked at Sonine's door. We heard him calling out:

"Sonine, Sonine, *please* don't be upset. We all understand what an embarrassing situation you were in, but you may be perfectly sure that your charming modesty has been preserved. . . The same misadventure happened to my dear Casimira, once. Her dress was caught in a revolving door in an hotel in Baden-Baden, and ripped to pieces," (naturally, this was a lie). . .

Sonine kept mum.

"Sonine," Grandfather went on, "you shall have as many petticoats as you wish, the most beautiful, the most costly. . . You may buy them whenever you like. . ."

After some time Sonine finally consented to come out of her room. She had adjusted her dress, and she walked as if her shoes were too tight and her feet were killing her. Her face showed all the signs of outraged dignity. I never knew whether she knew that we knew. . . We went back to our dinner, trying not to pay too much attention to her, and making painful efforts to carry on a conversation. Several times, Dæmon stared at Sonine. Sonine never met her eyes, and I felt, like a kind of surreptitious reminder, Dæmon's long tail beating against my leg. At one moment I nearly collapsed in giggles; at another I almost burst into sobs. And Dæmon kept on waving her tail about, and I didn't dare move for fear that Sonine might notice what was afoot under the table.

*

Naturally, my head was swimming. I spent all my time looking at Dæmon's tail. Then, when I was quite sure no one was watching me, I began to measure it. It had attained astonishing dimensions, which we pretended to be unaware of. Whenever anyone spoke of a swallowtail coat, or a dovetail joint, or of crayfish tails (they sometimes made us an exquisite cold soup of creamed cucumber and crayfish tails), I couldn't help jumping! Our ancient maid Theodosia, who had a huge, bushy beard, our no less ancient manservant Tolek, who used to dress up as a woman—and who sometimes used to forget to take off his makeup when he was serving at table (more than once some of our guests were shocked)—seemed to me like far-off creatures, barely if at all eccentric. In any case, they had left when Dæmon first began to manifest her authoritarian ways. . . In our remote regions, the ladies were baffled by the changing fashions, which were beyond their comprehension, and which anyway always arrived too late. Hence they dressed more or less at random, either following the sartorial customs of their ancestors, or merely following their own whims. When I saw Countess Hedwig's ample crinoline (she was the one who had fallen into the water at the time of the eclipse), I imagined that the purpose of its wide hoops was to support a tail that descended in spirals. When I stepped forward to greet the young Princess Irice who, for her part, wore a bustle under a dress with a train, I imagined that under the plump little cushion of the bustle there was the coiled-up fur of a tail. In short, I saw tails everywhere, even in my dreams. I began to believe that the saints cooped up in their niches in the churches were concealing furtive adjuncts. I got into the annoying habit of feeling my coccyx, to make quite sure that a caudal appendix wasn't growing there. . .

What had to happen, happened. . . Accompanied by Dæmon, who in such cases walked with the noiseless paws of a were-She-Cat, I started prowling around outside Sonine's room. I squinted at her door, kept walking up and down past it, humming absentmindedly, and then one day I could stand it no longer. Holding my breath, my heart thumping (I imagined I could hear a drumroll in the distance), I knelt down and put my eye to the keyhole. It was hearing sounds of water that had been the determining factor in this resolute, foolhardy gesture. And Sonine was indeed performing her ablutions, her feet immersed in a wooden tub. She was energetically scrubbing her broad back with a brush. She was a strapping wench, with a full figure, rounded hips, robust legs, enormous buttocks, but hers was a perfect rotundity. She was enthusiastically splashing water over herself, and under its constant stream her white skin shimmered like satin. Naturally, though, it was only her tail that fascinated me. It formed a kind of rigid arc of a circle, whose terminal plume was resting on the floor, like a friendly tame animal watching its mistress at her toilet. Every time a drop of water fell on its fur, the tail quivered, from which I deduced that it didn't much like water. After Sonine had thoroughly rinsed herself, she kept her arms upraised for a few moments, her body leaning slightly backwards, no doubt to dry herself. In this position I had the impression that she was being supported by her tail, in much the same way as sportsmen use shooting sticks, no doubt because they are exhausted by their ignoble carnage. But in actual fact, Sonine's tail represented everything that was pacific. I began to realize this, with some emotion. She took hold of it with one hand (which showed that she could make it flexible when she wanted to), and with the other hand she began to brush it for a long time. I could see her face looking at it with infinite tenderness. Then she combed it, she stroked it, and this charming intimacy between Baba, whom I had always found rather uncouth, and that tail, which was a highly uncommon, and no doubt horribly inconvenient appurtenance, brought tears to my eyes. When she had finished this operation, Sonine picked up a bottle with a rubber bulb attached to it and sprayed her tail. A whiff of perfume reached me, that I shall never forget, and that I shall never smell again anywhere: febrile, crepuscular, bitter-sweet, like the acrid odor of the fur of wild animals that have been rolling around in sweet-smelling flowering shrubs. . . I felt anxious, slightly sick, and I surrendered my place to Dæmon. Her eye widened and her pupil expanded and overflowed like thick, shiny ink, as black as mica. This mirror of the night, as I well knew, could see farther than I could; it plunged into shadows and mysteries that were none of my business. I guessed that in this instant a subtle, indestructible link had become established between Dæmon and Sonine. . . I took one last glance. Sonine's legs were slightly parted, still in the tub. Her upstretched arms were wringing out her long hair—and her tail was back in its initial position. I turned to Dæmon.

"It's very beautiful, though," I murmured.

"Yes," she replied.

She didn't speak, of course. But this reply didn't come from anywhere else. To make it, Dæmon didn't need to nod her head, to open her mouth, to articulate. She acquiesced, that was all. You only had to use your own feelings, and guess.

*

One evening there was a reception at the castle, in honor of Princess Irice, who was celebrating a false birthday. Surprisingly, Dæmon was seated opposite me. She kept looking at me. Sonine was sitting beside her. I was a bit bored, and, looking down, I caught a glimpse of a tuft of fur sticking out on my side of the long tablecloth, which came down to the ground. I was so flustered that I knocked over my glass (of champagne).

"Good luck, good luck," Irice cried inanely.

I took very little notice of her squawks and inept applause. I was in an agony of perplexity: *who* was sitting with her tail between her legs—or her paws—Dæmon or Sonine? How on earth could this tail reach under the whole width of the table and come and stick its muzzle—as you might say—out through the lace edging of the tablecloth? Were Dæmon and Sonine accomplices? Were they playing a trick on me? I was suffering martyrdom. . . Fortunately, we left the table, and Dæmon darted off, with a leap at least three meters long, pursued by a comet of hairs made glittering, flamboyant, almost sizzling, by all the disseminated candles, as if showers of sparks were flying in all directions from her dazzling fur. The "select" guests were dumbfounded. Princess Irice, who made a point of never being disconcerted (for her, this was proof of an aristocratic demeanour), declared, with a jaunty, frivolous air:

"But that charming creature's tail is divine. . ."

There was a silence, and then our Baba Sonine thundered:

"That's true. That's true, isn't it? Her tail is divine. . . like all tails. . ."

Her voice had taken on a terrible resonance; she pointed her avenging index finger at the terrorized princess and yelled:

"And you, Princess, you haven't, and you never will have, a tail!"

We danced attendance on the fainting Irice, and we

were just about to attribute Sonine's outburst to some slight seasonal mental aberration which no one should worry about, when Baba collapsed on to the settee in a fit of hysterical laughter. We followed suit: we couldn't keep a straight face. It was like the end of a game of "statues", when everyone suddenly comes to life again. We all fell over, roaring with laughter, to left, to right, one on to a chair, another on to an armchair (me, on the carpet). . . Dæmon was rushing around like a mad thing, and at one moment her tail coiled itself around the princess and nearly made her fall over. The princess flounced out in a huff, followed by the furious guests. . . And we laughed, we laughed, failing in all our duties! But what duties? What obligations? What was the meaning of those words?—we shouldn't even have known what they meant. We were all elated, as we stayed on in the deserted, flower-strewn salon, which was growing dark, for the candles were going out one by one. . . Grandmother Casimira, who had been the first to recover her composure, stood up very straight, and declared:

"A rare and sublime tail is infinitely preferable to the company of imbeciles. We shall never see them again. . . Adieu."

And she stretched out her arms to the windy night, with a queenly air. . . "Adieu. . . Adieu," we all chanted, as we went up to bed. What a charming word; "Adieu. . ." I went on repeating it for a long time, and I fell asleep peacefully, with Dæmon's tail curled around my neck, for I rather thought I had a slight sore throat.

# Desertions—We Don't Care: Frolics—We Like Them

*O*ur doltish domestics had left us (happily replaced by sprightly servants), and our visitors were becoming few and far between. The rumor had spread that we were now dominated by a Monstrous-and-Perverse-She-Cat; that we had become impossible to frequent; that a wind of folly was blowing over the castle—in addition to all the usual winds. . . We shrugged our shoulders. Our solitude was a privilege; why should we burden it with vain, futile mundanities? I often caught sight of Kinga on her way to the woods, escorted by a dashing-looking manservant. He would be carrying a big umbrella, some shawls, an easel—but I never, alas, saw the watercolors of the landscapes she described, with dreamy eyes. . . But she walked at a good pace, without the slightest affectation. As for Sonine, she cavorted with them all, both boys and girls; they only needed Dæmon to join in their merry games and then it was only too obvious that "There was great excitement in the air at the castle. . ."* Grandmother Casimira lost the thread of the passages she was reading; Grandfather Emeric got in a muddle with his collections. . . One day he called all the staff together and read them the riot act: some of the blushing maids had claimed to be pregnant, and despite the size of the castle I don't think he had any wish to turn it into a nursery. Besides, he detested babies: "frightful little squalling monkeys", he called them, "brought into the world to suffer or to cause suffering". . . Conferences were organized behind locked doors. I heard whispering and a few screams. . . In the end, the maids' stomachs remained nice and flat, and we didn't have any babies to baptise. . . They must have been lying, pretending to be brazen hussies, to make themselves interesting. . .

Naturally, a few curious acquaintances still made overtures to us. But we weren't fooled: they wanted to see Dæmon, her unbelievable size, to spy on us, and spread malicious rumors that we were a lot of hotheads, of King's jesters—that we were the sort of people you go and gape at in fairs. We treated them with icy reserve, and they never set foot in our domains again.

*

Nevertheless, there were still a few people with whom we remained on good terms—what you might
*Comtesse de Ségur, née Rostopchine.

call the survivors: friends who were flexible, tolerant, poetic, amusing and melancholic, like the Abbé Zygmunt, a plump, powdered man who resembled the obsequious abbés of the XVIIIth century, or like Countess Hedwig, who one day revealed herself in an unexpectedly comical light. She had herself announced, and came into the salon encircled by her inevitable crinoline (a lavender-colored one, if I remember rightly, covered with masses of powdery pompoms that were supposed to represent hollyhocks). . . Instead of coming up to us with a great show of dignity, as she usually did, she began to utter little cries, raised herself on tiptoe and arched her arms above her head like a ballerina. This irritated me no end. I thought she was putting on an eccentric act to try to demonstrate her connivance with us. We never indulged in such extravaganzas (not gratuitously, at any rate), and our faces were beginning to freeze when she whispered:

"Guess what I have under my dress?"

Sonine was present. . . I thought I was going to faint! If Countess Hedwig had had the preposterous idea of fabricating a false tail for herself, all we could do was retort that her joke was in the most doubtful taste, and thus put an abrupt end to our relations. . . But she went on hopping up and down, pretty nimbly I must say, given her embonpoint, and kept repeating:

"Guess, guess. . ." wagging a roguish index finger.

A solution had to be found. I concentrated, and tried, without too much imagination, to think of what conjurors' hats might conceal. In a glum voice, I said:

"Two or three white rabbits. . ."

"No no. . . Your turn, dear Casimira."

Grandmother too must have been thinking of the animals magicians use as props, and she said:

"A few doves or wood pigeons. . ."

"You're wrong. . . Let's ask Emeric."

She turned to Grandfather. He fidgeted in his armchair, gave a little cough, and, with obvious irritation, mumbled:

"Countess, I believe you are concealing nothing at all under your dress. . . It is my belief that you are playing a practical joke on us. . ."

He was getting worked up, but Hedwig was so absorbed in her antics that she took no notice of his somber air, looked at Kinga and asked her:

"And you, my child?"

Kinga took the trouble to pretend to be thinking, and because she liked fripperies which might, you never know, turn out to be presents, she asked:

"How should I know? Indian saris? Persian scarves? Creole gewgaws?"

"You're on the wrong track, too," said the countess, becoming more and more mischievous. "I ought to have asked for forfeits. . . We should have had such wonderful fun. . . The weather is so depressing!"

I was petrified. With all these absurd questions, and our laconic or grumpy answers, I had the feeling that we were becoming totally depraved. . . What were we all doing with this noble, highborn noodle? But the crucial moment arrived. Still posturing like a flirtatious, degenerate dancer, Countess Hedwig called out to our poor Baba:

"It's your turn, Sonine, and woe betide you if you're

wrong!'' Sonine's normally round face was transformed. It became violent, tense, its bones stuck out, it was the living image of fierce, furious rage. She eyed the countess disdainfully, and, with lightning in her eyes, thunder in her voice, and admirable courage, she flung at her:

"Countess, with your permission, I believe I know what you are concealing from us. . . A long, a very long hairy tail. . .''

Silence fell throughout the room, such an all-embracing, brutal silence that I had the impression that we were moving away from one another, that the furniture was receding, that the walls were disappearing. . . I felt I was being cast down through a gap in the sky, when the clouds suddenly part and reveal an infinite chasm beneath. . . But we pulled ourselves together, and, full of enthusiasm for our heroic Baba, we exclaimed:

"Bravo. Bravo. Sonine has won. . .''

For us, she was the victor. But the countess, who had remained speechless for quite a while, performed three little jumps, flung out her arms, and exclaimed:

"Sonine hasn't quite won. . . But it's rather extraordinary. She was far and away the nearest to the truth. Just look. . .''

Countess Hedwig lifted up her dress audaciously, and we saw Dæmon, who had slid under this silken airship like an amorous page hiding from the husband of a rather flighty lady. We were rooted to the spot. The countess dropped her skirts, but we kept on asking for a repeat performance, for the rare pleasure of watching this improvised curtain fall, and rise, fall, and rise on the astonishing and inventive Dæmon. "Encore. . .", "Encore. . .", we demanded, clapping our hands. But this indefinite raising of her heavy dress finally exhausted the countess.

"That's enough, my friends, *please*," she implored.

Dæmon took quite some time to extricate herself from the countess's crinoline, for her tail was wound around her legs, and its length, like that of her body— which was still growing and growing—would have terrified more than one poltroon. . . But Countess Hedwig had judged her to be just the right size to join in her frolics—and we were grateful to her. When she had finally emerged from all those furbelows, Dæmon shook herself (Countess Hedwig always left a heady trail of perfume behind her), and then sat down by her side. Both, with infinite grace, inclined their heads. We went on clapping—it had been a most charming interlude. . .

Naturally, Countess Hedwig stayed for dinner. We redoubled our praise, and both she and Dæmon seemed at once delighted and modest, like prima donnas after a magnificent aria. But secretly, it was Dæmon who was the real sensation. . . As for Baba, she had every good reason to gormandize, to down glass after glass of wine, champagne, and brandy. . . Had she not, after all, shown herself to be extraordinarily perspicacious?

# The-Lady-In-Black at the Inn in Barlskdat

Notwithstanding, Kinga and I (she was five years older than I) were really rather ignorant. Though we did know, thanks to Grandfather Emeric, about the flora and fauna. About the coleoptera—from the *Brachinus Crepitans* to the magnificent *Gerambyx Cerdo* -; about medicinal plants—from the marsh trefoil, which cured flatulent colics, to ground ivy, used against disorders of the bladder and kidneys. . . We read a great deal, and we wrote with a certain grace and facility. As was the case with all the aristocratic families of the region, we spoke several languages—we often used to converse in French, but we could express ourselves in German, in Hungarian, in Russian, and even in Italian, for we had been on several educational journeys. There had been several governesses at the castle. They had not stayed long (decidedly, the place lent itself to emigration), for after a few days they had all fallen very ill. Fräulein Penkenfen, who knew all Schiller's ballads by heart, had terrible hemorrhoids and heartburn. . . Miss Pelston, who put me through torture to make me sleep with my hands outside the sheet (Grandfather, when I complained to him, told her to leave me in peace), was covered in eczema and had terrible, toadstool-like polyps growing in her nose. "Serves her right," I thought, for I detested her. . . Mademoiselle Rémura, a Frenchwoman steeped in piety, spoke only in ejaculatory prayers, of the order of: "O Merciful Jesus", "O Virgin Mary", parroted day in and day out. . . Her prayers didn't do her the slightest bit of good, for not only did she have hemorrhoids, like Fräulein Penkenfen, but she was also subject to dropsy, convulsive coughing fits, flatulence, constipation, and then diarrhea. The poor woman, between two susurrations addressed to the heedless heavens, ended up in a state of total prostration caused by a tapeworm (she admitted to us the presence of this importunate animal, and, furthermore, complained of dreadful stitches in her side). None of these governesses was willing to believe in our decoctions, in our doctors or our veterinary surgeons, or in the old women of the region who, enveloped in their somber shawls, claimed to be something like witch-healers. . . It must be admitted that we didn't really encourage them to try any of these treatments, and we were always enormously relieved when we saw them packing their bags. They disappeared, like winds that had come to the wrong country, pale and bloodless, without a single backward glance at the castle—and yet we were politely waving our handkerchiefs.

*

We thought we had finally seen the last of these creatures when one day Grandfather announced:

"We have to go to the inn in Barlskdat, to fetch a lady. She has been recommended to me by Alexander" (who was my beloved uncle), "and she will, I think, make an excellent governess. . ."

I was worried. Kinga pleaded a dreadful migraine. Dæmon and Sonine disappeared. So I sacrificed myself and went with Grandfather in the barouche to the village of Barlskdat.

This was the first time in my life that I had set foot in an inn. I was surprised by the sobriety of the place: in the half-light (dusk was falling and the oil lamps weren't yet lit), I could just make out some massive tables, some benches, a few smallish objects—bottles, glasses. . . The general impression was of sadness and bareness. The only trace of decoration consisted of a few strings of garlic hanging from the ceiling. . . The inn was not deserted, but all the men and the two serving girls were grouped together in a corner, while at the far end, with her back to a fireplace in which there were a few dying embers, sitting on a stool, was a lady dressed entirely in black.

"Is that she?" I asked Grandfather quietly—and naïvely. . .

"Yes, I think so. . . Who else could it be?"

We went over to her in a profound silence, followed by the frightened eyes of the men and the two women, and then we bowed.

70

"I am Emeric Yenderloff, and this is my grandson, Max-Ulrich."

Strangely enough, the lady didn't answer. Not wishing to squirm like an idiot, I began to observe her. The first thing that struck me about her was that she seemed to be "enmeshed". And indeed, above her high, tightly-laced boots (she had her legs crossed in a rather audacious posture), I caught a glimpse of very fine-meshed stockings. Over her narrow, grogram sheath dress were superimposed what looked like tulle tunics; they reminded me of the nets we hung over the windows in the summer, to keep out all the pernicious insects and their accompanying miasmas. And it was difficult not to imagine insects caught in the mesh of a taut net when I contemplated her veil, with little black patches dotted all over it. Her hands were swathed in long filoselle gloves under which there were dazzling rings, like eyes behind Iberian blinds. In one of her hands was a long cigarette holder, from which a sinuous, bluish smoke was rising—Turkish, both in its movement and its odor. She let her cigarette burn, without bothering about it, and we were still standing there, motionless and mute, when she suddenly raised her veil. Her face, with its boldly-chiselled features and pointed chin, was a snowy white. But her dilated, jet-black eyes flashed with dazzling radiance, and her bright-red lips seemed to have been dipped in fresh blood. At last she decided to speak:

"It was very kind of you to come to meet me." (Her voice was hoarse, but very clear). "I am of British origin, but I can speak any language. I have had an eventful life, and I would prefer you not to know who I am. . . I knew Alexander," (here, for the first time, she drew on her cigarette holder and threw back her head) "and I loved him very much. . . But anyway, is he not lovable?"

We acquiesced politely.

"I shall not tell you my name," she went on, "and I would not like you to give me one. Call me Madame, if you wish. . . Or The-Lady-In-Black. I am, in a way, a widow. . ."

She burst into strident laughter, which made me jump; I heard a glass break in the lair of the frightened onlookers, then she quickly lowered her veil.

"And now, let us go. . ." she said suddenly, in authoritative tones.

We went. I was thinking of that laugh, of this widow, a Merry one, perhaps, and in my swaying head I silently hummed the "Waltz entrancing, Made for dancing All Night Long. . ." that my sister Kinga played on the piano, her head going round in circles, and sometimes with a dazed look, as if she had let herself be carried away by her musical merry-go-round that went on and on revolving, to the point of nausea. . .

When she arrived at the castle, Kinga, Sonine, Grandmother Casimira and Dæmon were waiting for her in the salon. The-Lady-In-Black stood still, and greeted everyone with great reticence. But when she was face to face with Dæmon, she said in a very clear voice:

"At last. . . I am really seeing her."

"Yes, that is She," we all chorused. . .

And I thought I saw her face quiver under her little veil.

72

We took her to her room. In the evening, at dinner, she appeared in a toilette fairly similar to that of the afternoon, but the tulle tunics over her inevitable grogram sheath dress had been replaced by chiffon panels, pleated, cut on the bias, and embroidered with black and gold flowers. I noticed that the black flies (or patches) on her veil had been transformed into tiny, scintillating ladybirds. . . When she ate, she barely raised her veil (she had removed her gloves, and her long, ivory-colored hands, covered in sparkling rings, looked as if they had been modelled out of pale wax.) It seemed to me, looking at her blood-red lips, that she was plunging her silver fork into a mouth that did not belong to her—an avid, venomous, animal mouth—, and her tongue, at one moment, looked downy and violaceous, like a putrefying flower. . . She spoke little. Sometimes about Warsaw, sometimes about Uncle Alexander. . . But she insisted, in the most natural way in the world, on Dæmon having a second helping of vegetables, and of the little chocolate and jam pastries. Before she retired, she turned to Dæmon, Kinga and me, and said:

"Tomorrow, we shall begin our lessons. . ."

*

We assembled in a little salon near Grandmother's study. The-Lady-In-Black sat down in a big armchair, facing Dæmon, Kinga and me, and then she began to speak:

"As you know, I am English. So I think we should start with that language, which you do not know. Since you clearly have a natural gift for speaking foreign tongues, I shall come straight to the point: I shall teach you 'Everyday Conversation'."

74

"Should we take notes?" I ventured, more out of politeness than interest.

"No, that would be a waste of time," she replied. "Just try and remember. . ."

And she began to throw in our faces, with total indifference, the most absurd sentences I had ever heard: "I would like a Baedeker. . .", "It is of the greatest utility to situate libraries in railway stations. . .", "The scenery is exceedingly quaint—and exceedingly insignificant. . .", "My overnight bag is missing. . .", "I cannot travel with my back to the engine without feeling greatly indisposed. . .", "Sir, when one is so sensitive, one reserves a private compartment. . .", "The locomotive has broken down; let us hope that another train is not coming up behind us. . ." Obviously it was a question of the inconveniences and incidents that occurred while travelling. I saw Dæmon yawn several times. Kinga was already dozing. . . As for me, I found long train journeys terribly boring. I suddenly fell asleep, and plunged into interminable British tunnels in which a soothing voice kept tirelessly repeating, in English: *"You can lie down, that does not trouble me"*; but I didn't learn what it meant until much later. . . A sound made us jump. The-Lady-In-Black had dropped the book she had been holding—she too had drowsed off. We all looked at each other, without the slightest embarrassment. I rubbed my eyes, and, still only half-awake, said:

"I believe we've arrived. . ."

Dæmon meowed, in an intonation which, in my state of torpor, I took to be an accent from across the English Channel. I could very easily imagine Dæmon meowing in English. . . We stretched ourselves. The-Lady-In-Black smoothed out the creases in her veil.

"What can you remember?" she asked vaguely.

"Absolutely nothing," we replied.

"You are quite right. . ."

She stood up, looked at herself in a mirror and arranged her hair, which had become somewhat ruffled while she was asleep, and then said:

"Tomorrow, whatever the weather, we shall go out and we shall do. . . some botany."

She made a slight movement which set her veils fluttering, tried out a dance step—or it could have been a skating step—and then left the room, bumping into the odd piece of furniture. The first lesson had turned into an excellent siesta—which wasn't so bad.

*

The next day, then, we went out to commune with nature. It hadn't been raining, but the sky was covered in a blanket of dark clouds. Baba, who was a strapping wench, was carrying our capes (including Dæmon's, which Grandmother had dreamed up, and had made in the conspiratorial style, for moonless nights), our boots, a few provisions neatly packed in a basket. We trudged along placidly. I was imagining a depressing enumeration of plants and flowers, then a picnic on the grass, and a little rural nap. I was already envisaging these lessons as the same old dreary round of apathy, the exchange of a few vague words, and quiet boredom. . . I hoped The-Lady-In-Black wouldn't catch any sort of ailment; I preferred—I very much preferred—her absentminded air of mourning to the jeremiads and troubles of the governesses who had preceded her. To show some semblance of interest, at one moment Kinga exclaimed:

"Look, there's a tormentil; the ideal remedy for jaundice."

The Lady showed no sign of emotion:

"I didn't know that," she said, in a faraway voice.

When we got to the edge of a wood, she looked around her and said:

"Why don't we sit here?"

Sonine put down her encumbrances, and then sat down on a little grassy promontory. Dæmon was sniffing suspiciously at a plant—a kind of daphne, I think it was—when the Lady suddenly emitted a piercing whistle, sprang forward, topsy-turvied, and stood on her hands, in which position she remained totally immobile.

"And can you do *that*?" she asked.

As she was under a curving branch, she looked like an enormous bat, to which diaphanous spiders' webs were clinging, and which had been through a hundred attics, a hundred caverns, before coming and hanging by its feet, on this tree, under our very eyes. . . She remained in this position for several seconds. We were staggered.

"That's called 'The Tall Tree', isn't it?" I enquired, just to say something.

The Lady, with her head upside down, her veil still somehow covering her face (I twisted my head, and those dark-shadowed eyes, that gauze over her lips, reminded me of an oriental acrobat), replied, in a very clear voice: "No. I call it 'the upside-down cary-atid'. . ."

She was still holding that difficult position, so, not wanting to be outdone, I did my best to imitate her. I collapsed, extremely inelegantly. I had a go at helping Kinga, trying to hold her ankles, but she kicked and struggled, and finally came crashing down with her nose in the grass. Dæmon, in her turn, made a courageous leap, and managed to support herself magnificently on her two front paws, facing the Lady, who did a backwards somersault and stood upright with surprising suppleness. Dæmon was still standing on her front paws, apparently effortlessly, and we congratulated her, and also the Lady, to whom we confessed:

"No one ever tried to teach us an exercise like that before."

"That was a mistake," she said, smoothing down her clothes a little. "We need to know how to do a great many useless things in life. That is often the only way to amuse ourselves."

Baba exclaimed:

"You're quite right. . . Take me, for example. . ."

But she had no time to continue. . . The Lady suddenly tore open her sheath dress (it must have been done up by snap fasteners), then began to rush down a grassy slope, hands outstretched, like a woman pursued. . . At one moment I thought she had stumbled, because her body suddenly seemed to have collapsed. No, though; she was merely doing, at incredible speed, what one usually calls "a cartwheel". In the chaos of her flying veils, I thought I could see a flight of dark-colored birds, unable to make up their minds to leave the ground, or a swirl of straggling wings being harried by a fierce animal. . . Then Dæmon, Kinga and I began to roll over on the grass, following the Lady, shrieking with joy. Sonine came running after us, yelling like a possessed rustic. The Lady told us that her acrobatic feat was called "the Malayan fan". . . We were overcome with admiration for her, for Dæmon, who matched her every invention, and for our own high spirits: all our actions seemed to follow one another perfectly naturally, and even though ours—except for Dæmon's—were pretty clumsy, it was nevertheless obvious that we were genuinely aching to lick the grass and the earth, to roll over in the puddles and the mud, to see the sky bespattered with clouds, the panicking branches scatter and multiply. . .

We went back to the castle, absolutely filthy. But Dæmon's coat was glossy and glistening with the vegetal humidity. I even believe she had grown some more (the exercises, no doubt), and she was perfectly clean, just like The-Lady-In-Black, who was also impeccable, apart from a few insects—real ones, this time— still stuck in her veil. Dæmon, who had jumped up on to a chest of drawers, undertook the task of removing them for her with great delicacy, with a claw that was like a mother-of-pearl crochet hook.

"But what on earth has happened to you?" Grandfather and Grandmother asked when they saw us in that state. . . Sonine had fallen over several times when she was running after us, and a bit of her skirt was still hitched up, revealing petticoats that had turned green, and were once again torn.

"We've been doing gymnastics," I replied.

"That's splendid, then," said Grandfather appreciatively.

These "turns", these acrobatics—I don't quite know what to call them—became more and more frequent. It is possible that our studies suffered because of them, but I realized that nature was entering into the very depths of my being. Kinga was becoming beautiful, and dishevelled—she looked like a luminous Ophelia—, and Dæmon filled the whole castle with the nostalgic aroma of the autumnal woods. . . Sometimes, when I was with her, I had the impression of sleeping on a bed of humus, of dead leaves, and her long hairs, which I caressed passionately, became those of all wild animals. She represented the sweet brutality of a certain world, the savage mystery of what takes place out there, behind the trees. I wonder whether she didn't perhaps go and seek out those animals, a long way away from the castle, near the ponds, whether she didn't rub her fur against their coats, her muzzle against their muzzles, and whether she didn't come back to us, to me, bearing with her their enigmas, their freedom, their fierce, protected purity. Yes, she was a messenger, who grew and grew as the leaves fell and fell.

The-Lady-In-Black taught us some contortions which were very difficult, but which made us very supple. She gave them strange, unusual names: "The whirlitwirl", the "crashspin", "the esparcarole". . . Some of the words must have been imported, as for instance "the Indian passepied" (I have already mentioned "the Malayan fan"), or the "Vira-Volta", *à la portugaise*. . . I used to read a great many French novels, in which people were always taking to the roads in gypsy caravans with no particular destination in view, and I could see myself as a trapeze artist, I imagined Kinga as a tightrope dancer, Sonine exhibiting her tail, The-Lady-In-Black enigmatically sticking out her tongue, and Dæmon as a fabulous animal who at the same time dazzled and terrified the audience, merely by walking once around the ring, slowly and disdainfully, but making a spectacular exit, pirouetting furiously, between two purple curtains which swallowed her up at one stroke.

I very much appreciated The-Lady-In-Black, her abstracted airs, her silences, her grace, and her inestimable gift for leaving us in peace. I liked her clothes, and the way she wandered up and down the corridors, often accompanied by Dæmon. They sometimes took tea alone, in the conservatory where rare species of trees were grown, as well as tortuous, decorative plants, which seemed to be leaning over the Lady and Dæmon in an attempt to discover their secrets. I used to spy on them, and I would often hear the Lady speak of Warsaw, of Alexander—and Dæmon would incline her head in an understanding, meditative way. . .

*

The Lady loved the dramatic paintings in the entrance hall. One day, in the course of our peregrinations, she began to talk about earthquakes and floods. By chance she had found in her room a pile of the newspapers Mademoiselle Rémura—our former

French governess—used to have sent to her, which triumphantly announced national catastrophes, cataclysms, state funerals (I believe the paper was called *l'Univers*). The Lady combined these calamities with her tales of the torments of the heart and of life. . . She went on to speak of expeditions to the Poles, where at least one is not at the mercy of disastrous waltzes, of Polonaises, or Malagueñas, and without realizing it we found ourself in the very heart of a damp forest where we could hear rippling sounds. The farther under the trees we went, the more spongy the ground became. Fortunately, Baba hadn't come with us—she might have got bogged down. Dæmon preceded us, with a feline assurance that forced the most thickset grass, the densest scrub, to part. We were bathed in a greenish twilight, our lips were blue with the berries we smeared over them, just to feel their powdery velvet, and the brambles tore The-Lady-In-Black's veils. Quite unconcerned by such snags, she went on telling us about the bizarre vegetation she had come across during her innumerable journeys (buck's horn plantain, tocaris, pama-trees), and about the dangerous glimpses she had caught of animals conjured up by the shapes of the rampant roots, the rotting tree trunks (jaguars, tapirs, cobras). . . Higher up, in the branches, the gleaming leaves had invented exotic birds. . . and the Lady told us about parrots, parakeets, macaws. . . Our outing had become an expedition into the jungle, and we listened agog to The-Lady-In-Black, while the clearings narrowed and the trees converged. Soon we were plunged into the perpetual night of the primeval forests, and the ground began to move, to breathe, and we heard the bark cracking on the trees, the poisonous berries bursting, a wild stampede. . . Our hearts were galloping so fast that suddenly, without realizing it, we passed from one continent to another. The shades of night had exiled us, our breath was glacial, and we caught a glimpse of a lake which made us forget all about the Tropics and brought us back to our earlier polar expeditions. It was grey and silvery and looked as if it was frozen over. Great floating branches presaged the first ice floes. On the bank, a little boat was slowly rotting away. Without even consulting each other, we took it. Dæmon installed herself in the bows of the fragile, leaky craft; The-Lady-In-Black sat in the stern. Kinga and I tried to row it with its worm-eaten oars (and anyway, Kinga's oar broke.) Nevertheless, we managed to reach the middle of the lake, and we realized that it was reflecting a low sky, the portent of the first snows. We didn't speak. Dæmon was staring straight ahead of her, like a lookout, in the superb immobility of a figure-head carved in the form of a Great-Marine-She-Cat, and what remained of the Lady's torn, straggling veils floated on the surface of the water. At one moment Kinga broke the silence and announced that she was sure she was going to have an attack of colic from eating that noxious fruit. I asked her to keep quiet, and just look. . . And that was when I began to be frightened. Everything was whirling around inside me like a tornado, the Jungle and the Pole, Dæmon and The-Lady-In-Black. We had gone too far in our expedition, and what I saw then I shall never forget. The Lady had raised her veil and thrown her head back a little. Her tongue came out of her mouth, and it was infinitely longer than I had imagined. It was covered in a frothy film that reminded me of the fluffy layer of mold on jam going bad. It was obvious that it was attracting the insects, which alighted on it and then found themselves limed. I could see their wings flapping, and the Lady's eyes resting on them with magnetic cruelty. She waited a moment; then, with a frightful smacking sound, she swallowed them, and then once again stuck out her terrifying appendage— it was violaceous, as I had several times briefly glimpsed, but it was also covered in bluish spots. Horrified, I turned round to Dæmon, who hadn't budged. The trunks that looked like caimans were bending over her, and frogs on glossy, silky leaves were fascinated by her. All those shimmering ripples converging in her direction formed a kind of ever-widening fan of mercury on the water. Kinga was chanting what must have been a gypsy song, and then she began to vomit. Every time the boat lurched, my heart missed a beat. My head was swimming. I thought I was going to faint as our craft slowly, gently, inexorably, sank into the lake. I had plenty of time to think: Life is short. . .

# Uncle Alexander's Visit

. . . *B*ut we didn't drown, for the lake was very shallow. We got back to the castle in such a pitiable state that Grandmother Casimira and Sonine—who had been grumbling all day because we had gone without her—fainted. We had to take to our beds, and the doctor, urgently sent for, predicted pneumonia for both Kinga and me. . . Fortunately his diagnosis turned out to be mistaken. Neither Dæmon nor the Lady, who appeared the next day adorned in black spangled feathers, so much as sneezed. They came to my bedside. The Lady read me some witty little poems, and I think Dæmon cured me when she lay at full length beside me, covering me with all the warmth of her soft, feathery fur.

From my bed, I looked out of the window and watched the first snowflakes falling. Dæmon had gone to sleep by my side. The Lady had put down her book. I could see that the winter was approaching, that the silence of the snows was about to envelop us, and that the castle was going to become a little more delightfully self-sufficient. . . Suddenly I heard cries, and the distant jingling of little bells that heralded a barouche. Sonine came rushing into the room and I nearly fell out of bed.

"He's coming," she shouted, panting.

"Who?. . ." I asked the question for the pure pleasure of hearing the answer, that name.

"Why, Alexander. . . Come on, Max-Ulrich, don't pretend. . ."

I wanted to get up but Sonine held me back by force, and rather spitefully, I must say. The entrance hall had become, it would appear, the very crossroads of every conceivable draught, and several of the manservants and maids were also ill in bed. A great deal of coughing went on in the corridors. The minutes ticking by seemed interminable. At last he came in. My Uncle Alexander was just as he always had been: tall, slender, graceful, a Varsovian to the tips of his slightly curved mustaches. He was the only one in the family to have light-colored eyes—blue, green, grey—always changing. He threw himself on me, pulled me out of bed, twisted me around—and he was already nibbling at my neck with his pointed teeth. Soon the room was invaded by the animals that followed him everywhere: two leverets, a monkey dressed in a little gold-embroidered bolero, and some white cockatoos which began energetically pecking at the legs of a table. He spread out the presents he had brought me. In a frenzy, I ripped off the wrapping paper and ribbons, and uncovered albums containing drawings he had done of handsome young men, and sinuous women (who all resembled The-Lady-In-Black). Then I saw some books—not very respectable ones, but highly instructive—and some very eccentric, silky garments which came from Nowy Swiat Street. Finally, his manservant appeared, carrying, with impressive solemnity, a gramophone with a horn, and Alexander immediately put on a record of a czardas whose slow, undulating start, with its pent-up tension, I found deeply disturbing. I was listening to the melodies of the violins, which were extended like long, benumbed arms, when Alexander went up to the Lady. . .

"I saw you at once, of course. I knew you were here, my dear, dear friend. . ."

She held out her hand; he took it, kissed it. . .

"Dear Alexander," she murmured (for the first time I heard a dying fall in her voice—at the same time as that of the languid melody. . .) He moved his face closer to hers, and I was a little surprised that she didn't raise her veil. But perhaps the shadow of the gauze increased their intimacy. They remained like that for a few seconds, until the moment when the violins went wild. . . I took advantage of this to give a little cough, and to say:

"Dearest Uncle Alexander, you're forgetting Dæmon. . ."

"I saw her, too, the moment I came in. . . She is beauty incarnate. . . But she was asleep. . ."

"She isn't asleep now. . ."

Dæmon, in fact, was stretching on the bed. Alexander went up to her. They stared at each other, and then, when my uncle was very close to her, she leaped forward and placed her two paws on his shoulders. He staggered a little, given her size and weight, but his face, which was already radiant, became even more so. I was witnessing a noble accolade; noble, but infinitely tender.

"She likes you," I exclaimed, wild with joy.

"And I like her," Alexander replied. "I love her, I love her madly."

The music accelerated, and everyone in the room rushed over to my bed. They all threw themselves on me and Dæmon. . . Sonine, the Lady, and Alexander embraced us, and while the vertiginous violins went on whirling, we all sobbed with passion and bliss.

Naturally, we gave a party. Countess Hedwig arrived in a puce-colored crinoline so wide that she had to come in through one of the bay windows in the conservatory. The Abbé Zygmunt was invited; he was followed by a young seminarian, Grigori, who went everywhere with him, and who swung his hips when he walked, like certain young men in certain streets in the Capital. . . The dinner was superb. Alexander declared that since Dæmon didn't go in for fancy manners, since she lapped things up with the greatest simplicity, and grasped all the food put in front of her with her expert claws, we didn't need knives and forks either. He threw his own (with their extremely complicated emblazoned handles) over his shoulder. We followed suit, and ate very practically with our fingers, licking them frequently. As was right and proper, Dæmon called the tune, and we all belched and farted with enthusiasm. At the end of the meal there was an incident that might have been serious. The Abbé Zygmunt's face turned purple. He clutched his chest, choked, and declared:

"I think I'm going to have a stroke. I feel as if I'm going to explode. Quick, quick, I need a corset. . ."

Sonine rushed out and brought back one of hers. We imprisoned him in his constrictive prop, and his acolyte, Grigori, laced him up, uttering poignant cries. The Abbé seemed to have stopped breathing. . .

"O Virgin Mary, O God, forgive me or don't forgive me, it doesn't much matter which. . . But cure me, for pity's sake," he said, as if these were his last words.

We laid him down on a sofa, very gently. He shut his eyes, and then his face gradually brightened and he began to smile. . .

"It's over. It was just a passing malaise. Oof! Oof! Oof!. . ."

He mopped his brow, and Grigori deftly removed Sonine's corset. The Abbé Zygmunt leaped up and cut a few capers, to make it quite clear that he was back on his feet. . . The servants sang, beat on tambourines, and the Abbé launched out into a lively dance, partnered by Grigori, who had gone quite pink with excitement.

We played tag (which the French call "Chat", and the Polish call "Berek".) Grandfather and Grandmother, who were feeling a little weary, remained seated. They were content to lift their feet off the ground when the hunter approached. As usual, Sonine tripped over a rug and got herself caught, waving her arms around wildly. Kinga never stopped running, even when no one was chasing her. Grigori was squealing, and at one moment, to escape me, he jumped up on to the back of one of the servants, whose tambourine went rolling away like a hoop with bells. . . Alexander was very nimble and stylish. Naturally, Dæmon and The-Lady-In-Black were untouchable. I was enjoying myself enormously, and I adored the moments when Dæmon was chasing me. Even though it was against the rules to leave the salon, at one moment I couldn't stop myself taking flight, with Dæmon on my heels. I ran until I was out of breath, and then took refuge in a dark corner of a corridor. My heart beating furiously, I had time to see her coming nearer, her eyes as bright as flares. She slowed down, pretended she hadn't seen me, and then abruptly turned around and hurled herself on me, terrified and abandoned as I was, and placed her paws on my shoulders, as she had done to Alexander when they were introduced. I realized then that she was as tall as I was. I kissed her on her muzzle, putting an arm around her neck. . .

Countess Hedwig had to pay a forfeit: she had to turn herself into a cushion. She did so with good grace; she crouched down and tucked her head into her enormous puce crinoline. Mischievously, Dæmon jumped up on to her back and nonchalantly stretched out on that mass of rippling, rustling materials. The countess bore this ordeal valiantly—we applauded like anything. . .

The best moment, no doubt, was when the Abbé Zygmunt, pursued by Dæmon, jumped up on to a little table with surprising agility. Maybe his ecclesiastical situation provided him with invisible wings. But the fragile little table couldn't take his weight, and it collapsed with an ear-splitting din. The Abbé fell heavily to the ground, yelling a word that had certainly been whispered in his ear by some perfidious devil ("Piorum!"). Grigori flung himself on him, and we all rushed up in a great state of agitation. Luckily, the Abbé was laughing, and hadn't hurt himself. We drew the conclusion that his fall was an excellent punishment—and with that, our frolics came to an end.

It was very late. The snow had been falling without a break, and it was already very thick on the ground. I imagined that an aurora borealis would look like that: the slightly fluorescent blue of the sky, and the infinite whiteness stretching out under my sleepy eyes. And anyway, the dawn must have broken. . . The guests had to stay the night at the castle. We showed Countess Hedwig—who was asleep on her feet and who moved as if she had roller skates underneath her devastated crinoline—to the bedroom with the grey-silk tapestried walls (which couldn't fail to harmonize with her toilette). . . The Abbé Zygmunt and Grigori wanted to share a room, so as not to be a nuisance. We didn't feel up to telling them that the castle had so many rooms—fifty, or even more. . . I was tottering with fatigue. Dæmon, at least, didn't need to undress. I collapsed on to the bed, my Nowy Swiat Street clothes scattered all over the floor. Dæmon was already asleep—but she moved closer to me, while I buried myself, I think, in her fur. . .

*

At that time, there were rumors of war. We took no notice of them, not out of indifference, or egoism, but out of simple horror. But whispers spread among the servants and the peasants. The headlines in the newspapers became bigger and began to drip with hatred, and two or three times we caught a glimpse of enormous, shiny metal birds in the sky—the first airplanes I had ever seen. . .

One day, a kind of swashbuckler turned up at the castle, a repulsive, arrogant man, who announced to Grandmother Casimira in an authoritative voice:

"It is my duty, Madame, to requisition all the males in the castle and the village. . ."

Grandmother didn't flinch. She received him in the entrance hall, while Dæmon, who happened to be there with me, began to growl. She advanced on the mercenary; he retreated in cowardly fashion.

"A beautiful animal," said the horrible soldier, in a wavering voice.

"She is not an 'animal'," Grandmother stated in disgust, throwing her lorgnette into the tray with the spectacles. . . "I must tell you, sir, that here there are only maidservants. . . As for the village, it so happens that it is a village of women. It is strange, but that is how it is. Their babies must be born and conceived in the woods. . . I do not know, and I do not make it my business to know. . . I am extremely sorry, but you will find no cannon fodder in this vicinity."

Grandmother stamped her foot. The soldier shook in his shoes. But he went on:

"I am under an obligation to return, three days from now, to make sure of these facts, which do indeed seem strange. . . My respects, Madame."

He clicked his heels and departed, while Grandmother turned her back on him in disdain. So did Dæmon, with her fur standing on end like the wild grass in the park—when it wasn't snowing. . .

I hurried off to look for Alexander, and found him on his knees in front of The-Lady-In-Black. The gramophone was playing "The Mountain Shepherd". I told him what had just happened and I began to cry, because I didn't want our delightful servants to leave us, lined up like soldiers, with guns over their shoulders. . . Alexander thought for a few seconds, and then declared:

"I see only one solution. We must dress the men up as women. . ."

He summoned all the castle staff, and the servants seemed overjoyed by this winter carnival. The peasants from the village, who had got wind of what was going on, were already on their way to the castle, their shoulders drooping, their eyes imploring. We told them what we had just decided. They let out great shouts of joy, and some of the more excitable ones threw themselves down at Grandmother's feet. She said:

"Come come, my good men, no flummery if you please. . . You must get to work, you and your wives, and in three days' time, come back here. We shall say 'No' to war." (It must be admitted, though, that as she pronounced these words Grandmother made an extremely warlike gesture.) The peasants departed, jubilant, singing old folk songs from the district that their joy had resuscitated.

*

I was in such a state of nervous excitement that I got a slight temperature. To take my mind off things, no doubt, Alexander decided to fire a salute. He led me and Dæmon and The-Lady-In-Black over to a cluster of very old cannons, that had never defended anything and were rather chaotically disposed at some distance from the castle. No one knew how they had got there, and even though we didn't attach the slightest importance to them, we hadn't taken the trouble to get rid of them. Covered with snow as they were, they looked like so many statues of Cerberus, on the watch. . . Alexander, who liked fireworks and detonations, knew how to make two or three of them operational. He put a cannonball into an opening, busied himself with all this and that, and then announced:

"Look out; I'm ready."

I was just about to stop my ears when I heard a distant humming sound. A dazzling speck appeared in the grey sky: a passing airplane. I saw Dæmon's eyes distending, and The-Lady-In-Black snatching off her veil with a furious hand. Her downy tongue kept passing over her lips from left to right. . . The airplane was coming nearer. . . Dæmon crouched down as if getting ready to spring.

"I'll exterminate it," said Alexander, laughing.

He lit his fuse, and waited. . . There was an explosion, but rather a disappointing one, even though it aroused an echo—followed by a sparkling geyser of snow. Alexander was buried under a shower of black powder. The cannonball made its way slowly upward, and then suddenly plummeted, like a big, clumsy bird that hadn't managed to spread its wings. I was thinking that my uncle was giving himself a lot of trouble for nothing when I saw the airplane falter in the skies. It seemed to be lost, to be bumping into the clouds. It began to quiver, and give fitful little coughs. It went around in a circle four times, and then did a nose dive, streaking through the sky like a skate across the ice. We didn't flinch, we went on contemplating the clouds, probably thinking that the airplane would very soon start climbing again, as a sort of response to our game. But the forests, the marshes, or whatever, had swallowed it up forever. The snowflakes began to fall again, and when I cast an eye on the innocent cannonball it was already covered in snow—it seemed to be hiding in fright. Dæmon, looking immense, went over to it with a sure paw, walked around it, barely sniffed at it, and then went off towards the castle. We followed her, talking about the weather in an absentminded sort of way. In the entrance hall, I ventured to say:

"Even so, some coincidences. . ."

"That's life," the Lady cut me short.

Dæmon was shaking herself, and Alexander, who looked like a chimney sweep, was dusting himself down. . .

"Yes," he went on. "Life is full of ups and downs. . ." (He gave a little laugh.) "We know something about that, don't we, my Dear?"

The Lady smiled at him and patted his cheek. I was soon quite certain that the airplane had made a great mistake in passing that way—and I began to stroke Dæmon, who was singing, and in an excellent mood.

Alexander couldn't hold his tongue (he was very garrulous), and he related everything that had happened. An agitated peasant came and announced that a machine had fallen into a lake. Dæmon gave a sort of hiccup. . . Later, a few more airplanes flew over the castle or its environs. They irritated Grandmother, and Grandfather mumbled: "Hm, there's a storm in the air. . ." But quite soon they changed their flight path, and we forgot them.

*

Nevertheless, I did begin to reflect for a few instants on accidents and their irrelevance, but the perpetual comings and goings in the castle gave me other things to think about. We had to turn our attention to the disguises. We went up into the attic, opened some trunks full of dust and the lingering traces of old, sad scents, and Dæmon frantically extracted dresses, petticoats, and masses of materials and gewgaws. Grandmother Casimira, Kinga, Sonine and the maidservants were already plying their needles. The-Lady-In-Black added bits of flashy costume jewelry everywhere. Grandfather Emeric, with the help of Alexander, who had exquisite taste, gave excellent advice. I went from one to the other carrying threads, bodkins, and fairly useless bits of embroidery. The fittings began. Kinga was fussing over the curly-haired, gypsy-like lad who used to carry her easel to the woods before the snows began. Sonine was in a flat spin; at one moment she declared that she was sorry she wasn't a boy—because she couldn't turn herself into a girl! I asked her whether she would like to disguise herself as a man.

"Yes," she replied, "I'd simply adore to."

I imagined her wearing boots, and silk breeches with a hole in them for her long tail to come through. This idea set me dreaming, but Grandmother called me to order.

"Come on, Max-Ulrich, we have no time to lose; pass me that belt." She put it around the waist of a servant standing in front of her with his arms up, and she must have tickled him because he began to giggle rather stupidly.

Alexander, The-Lady-In-Black, Dæmon and I went to the village to get an idea of the lie of the land. All the women were at work by their firesides. . . Not a single beard was floating in the breezes of the advancing winter. We saw some comic-looking men cutting wood, wearing women's long shifts. Others were shovelling snow, draped in embroidered fichus. We didn't know whether to say: "Good morning, gentlemen," or "Good morning, ladies"—so we concluded that everything was going extremely well. We were greeted everywhere with exclamations of joy. But we witnessed a few flights of fancy. Certain individuals, no matter what their age, insisted on their blouses being in perfect harmony with their skirts and flowered aprons. Their wives seemed puzzled—and even irritated. Perhaps they themselves had never given much thought to the important question of color-matching.

At last the day for the conscription arrived. We saw a sizeable procession of murmuring women coming up to the castle. . . As it wasn't snowing, braziers were lit, and the petticoated village lined up on the left of the castle steps. The menservants—or rather, the maidservants (we no longer knew which were which)—stood on the right. We were stationed at the top of the steps, well wrapped up (Dæmon was wearing her cape, for it was terribly cold), when the military man and his squad appeared. In the profound silence, he bowed, and, addressing Grandmother and Dæmon, who represented the sovereign ladies of our realm, he proclaimed:

"Mesdames, we came through the village, and it was deserted."

"Sir," Grandmother replied, in an extremely clear, deliberate voice, "the women were afraid of the rapacious and licentious soldiery. No doubt they were right; they have taken refuge with us. . . They are here." She waved a hand to her left and, as one man, the whole village hung its head. A few giggles could be heard, and the sinister ambassador could not refrain from a little persiflage:

"My goodness, there are some saucy little wenches in these parts. . ."

He wasn't given time to continue. Grandmother interrupted him, pointing to her washerwomen, cooks, chambermaids, and lady's maids:

"As for my own dear domestics—they are here. . ." On this side too, we became aware of some imperfectly stifled laughter—and I saw Dæmon's flanks quivering under her cloak: she must have been having a fit of the giggles. I myself had to bite the inside of my cheeks, to keep myself in check.

98

The soldier seemed confused. He brought a hand up to his forehead and declared:

"Mesdames, I am obliged to face facts. I see no one here but delightful members of the fair sex. . . If you will allow me. . ."

He paraded slowly in front of the assembled village, and I was amazed to see so many cheeks blush, so many eyelids lower, so many heads bow, with obvious coquetry. . . He went over to our servants, began to contort his lips in a ghastly grin, and pinched the chin of a young man (I had put my glasses on and I recognized Kinga's favorite), who took a step backward and hid his face in his bent arm. . .

"Adorable. . . Adorable. . ." he murmured. He cleared his throat, flung out his arms, and declared:

"Mesdames, all that remains for me to do is to leave you in this charming company. I have set eyes on some most agreeable young ladies, who would make perfect canteen women. . . But I suppose. . ."

"That's enough, sir," Grandmother said angrily. "I think it is time for you to take your leave."

"Indeed," he averred. "I apologize for putting you to so much trouble. . ."

He draped himself in his cape with infinite distinction. He shot one final glance at the groups that so captivated him—and I have to admit that the look of disillusion that passed over his face rendered him almost human. . . He departed, with his suite. When they were sufficiently far away, everyone began to laugh, and sing, and dance in the snow. These manifestations may seem repetitive, but I personally am convinced that happiness can only show itself in gyrations and gesticulations. . . A light meal was served. Both transvestites and others drank a great deal, but the rejoicings became somewhat vitiated when some of them began to lift up their skirts and embrace one another passionately. But given such merrymaking, why not enjoy it to the full. . . ?

Later, when they had all staggered off, arm in arm, Grandmother Casimira said:

"I enjoyed myself. I had the impression that I was a kind of Erzsébet Báthory, but a rather more peace-loving one, even so. . ."

I ought to say that Erzsébet Báthory was a Hungarian countess of great beauty who had the unfortunate habit of massacring very young girls and taking warm baths in their blood. . . But after all, everyone to his own fantasies. . .

*

Apropos of fantasies, there are some people who scratch their noses, their foreheads, their heads, or who stick their fingers in their ears or in their nostrils, or even in their behinds. . . As for my dear Uncle Alexander, he used to sharpen his teeth with a delicate silver file. He would indulge in this activity absent-mindedly, looking just like people do when they are polishing their nails. . . He had white, extremely pointed teeth—two in particular—and he could make them project over his lower lip if he wanted to. This gave him a bizarre, not to say disquieting expression. I must admit that I didn't in the least object to their acute contact, especially when we were enjoying ourselves playing "Gra", (the "Game"), a sort of hide-

and-seek-chase for two, which consisted of my running away and hiding somewhere until Alexander
found me. To make it quite clear that he had flushed
me, he would start growling like a wild animal and
fling himself on me, nipping my neck with his sharpened teeth. Afterwards, I often felt weary. . . He admitted to me that he sometimes played this game,
which greatly amused him, in other castles, and more
than once I caught myself feeling jealous of his
partner—whether male or female. One evening,
"Gra" nearly came to a bad end. We had just finished
dinner, and we all declared that we felt very tired. This
general lassitude may well have been due to all the
activities caused by the visit of the soldier, to all the
festivities organized by Alexander on the slightest pre-
text, or quite simply to the snowstorm raging out-
doors, a storm accompanied by a howling wind and
violent thunderclaps, which shook the castle to its
foundations. We felt like taking refuge in our bedrooms, and everyone went up to bed. Even The-Lady-
In-Black, who was usually more of a nocturnal dispo-
sition and who, it seemed to me, had just had an
argument with my uncle, in a corner of the room,
about a somber story of something that had happened
to them in a remote castle in the Carpathians. . . And
even Dæmon, who, when she reached the door, looked
over her shoulder imperiously to see whether I was
following her. . .

"I'll be up in a moment. . . I'll stay with Alexander
a little longer. . ."

I uttered these words with some embarrassment. I
hated to be parted from her, even for a few instants,

and especially when she enjoined me like this to follow her. Strictly speaking, our relations were not those of master and slave, they were of a rather undisciplined nature. I liked to obey her, for with her, submission had nothing in common with servility: it was more like a joyous, passionate impulse, which gave a welcome boost to the rate of my only-too-regular heartbeats. . .

Alexander and I were alone, then, in the deserted salon. A few candles had already gone out, and, as we became progressively enveloped in the pale, pleasant, semi-darkness, the wind—which seemed to be possessed of fangs and horns—was battering the windows, and the snow was buzzing as if the castle were being invaded by a swarm of pernicious insects. Between two squalls, I had the impression that feverish legs, ruffled wings, were interminably rubbing themselves against the windowpanes, which would eventually disintegrate—a disintegration that might well become fatal to us. . . Alexander was listening to all these sounds with a dreamy air. He was drinking Starka, whose amber color I found fascinating. He made the mistake of offering me some, and I made the mistake of accepting it. A few minutes elapsed. Before long my cheeks were on fire, and the agony of the wind, the abrasion of the snow's wings, seemed to become intensified. . . I threw my glass into the fireplace, something I had often seen done. Almost immediately my Uncle Alexander's glass joined mine. It must still have had some Starka in it, for the dying embers suddenly blazed up, and in the ruddy glow of the flames I saw his expression change, become both fixed and feverish, while his eyes grew larger, and his sharpened teeth appeared. Alexander was observing me—without seeing me, I thought—with such intensity that I began to feel ill at ease. I had the impression that he thought me guilty of a sin I hadn't committed, and I was beginning to fidget on my chair when he stretched out an arm to me:

"Would you like us to play. . ." he hesitated for a moment, as if he found the word difficult to say—"'Gra'?"

"Oh yes! Do let's play. . ."

I tried to put some enthusiasm in my voice, but what I actually felt was fear, and I was wondering: Why this game so late in the evening, why that drink I had had, and why this castle, gently bobbing up and down on the languid waves of the snow? I stood up eagerly. Alexander was still staring at me, and, even though the flames had died out, I thought I could glimpse an angry impatience in his expression.

"I'll give you three minutes to hide, then," he announced brutally.

I disappeared, trying not to bump into any of the innumerable pieces of furniture in the salon. The wind was blowing in my ears, now; it was propelling me, and even though I ran until I was out of breath, the rugs, the stairs, had turned into snow. . . I plunged into a fleecy universe, it was like one of those dreams where you're running away from a pursuer. . . I found myself in the attic, where I was magnetically drawn to the windowless skylight on whose ledge Dæmon had appeared to me. How I regretted her absence, at that precise moment! Snowflakes were drifting about like frothy flowers. . . I moved forward, and as I watched the snow I had the feeling that the sky was interminably disintegrating, falling, whereas the attic was floating upwards into the air. For a moment I believed myself to be on a flying platform, and as I went on ascending I experienced a kind of nausea. . . I vomited into a copper bowl that happened to be there, and then, feeling better, I remembered the "Game", and the time that had elapsed. I hurried over to the ghosts of the furniture, which quickly surrounded me, and I slid behind a long, low settee. I huddled up, because I was cold. Soon, I heard the attic door creak. I realized my mistake. I should never have hidden at the top of the house, in the midst of the forgotten things and their shrouds, too close to that glacial night which was still rumbling in the distance, perhaps over by the hills, I no longer knew, my heart was thumping so hard. I believe Alexander heard my uncontrollable heartbeats, and I listened, terrified, to the sound of his feet bringing him in my direction. The space between us was narrowing. . . And my terror increased. My uncle was purposely walking slowly, to frighten me even more, no doubt, but he didn't for a single moment pretend to hesitate. He was inexorably coming towards me, and in any case the skylight through which the cold and the snow were coming, the whiteness of the dustcovers of the ghost-furniture, the certainly perceptible odor of my disgorgement, could only draw him on. . . He soon came to a halt, and I knew he was very near me. It's odd; at that moment there was a silence, and I realized that it was impossi-

ble for any sound to come out of my mouth. I bit my wrist cruelly, I waited, I saw my Uncle Alexander's face leaning over me. I wanted to say: "No. . . no. . .", but my lips remained sealed. Only the erratic metronome of my heart told me that I was still alive. I felt the sickly sweet taste of my blood on my tongue, and I abandoned myself, my head thrown back. . . Alexander took me by force. I was inert between his arms, which were squeezing me, and I had the impression that I had become weightless, incapable of reaction, that I belonged to the mortal indolence of the snow. . . I shut my eyes. My uncle picked me up, and I felt a violent pain. He had brutally implanted his teeth in my neck. They remained embedded there, while I sank into the cold, the ice, and the deepest of all nights.

I must have fainted. I came to, later, in my bed. I was so totally exhausted that I had difficulty in raising my eyelids. My eyes turned to Dæmon, who was watching over me, and I think the enlarged, coppery suns of her gaze revived me a little, and comforted me. I saw, floating above me, the faces of Grandmother Casimira, Grandfather Emeric, Sonine, Kinga. . . They succeeded one another, and in their rapid, tremulous progression they looked like rather fuzzy photographs. I thought they were all dead, and at one moment I wondered whether I wasn't looking through the album of their pasts. Dæmon was the only one who seemed real. She was sitting by my side in the pose of the vigilant sphinx, and I managed to stretch out a hand and touch one of her warm paws. At last I heard voices:

"We must go for the doctor," Grandmother was imploring.

"There's so much snow, he won't get here until tomorrow," Grandfather replied.

"Perhaps a good enema and a few leeches," Baba suggested.

I heard sobs. Poor Kinga, who had nothing to offer, had dissolved into tears. . .

"We must quite simply cure Max-Ulrich ourselves, here and now, this instant. . ."

It was Alexander speaking. His voice, which he was trying to keep steady, couldn't help trembling and quavering. Then I remembered "Gra" (or the "Game"—whichever you like), and I realized that he had a guilty conscience. He came up to me. His face was pale, and rather grey. He seemed sad and imploring. He placed an arctic hand on my forehead, and at the contact of this glacial palm I realized that I, in contrast, had become a little warmer, and that Alexander was begging for indulgence. I smiled at him tenderly, but Dæmon, who was staring at him with cruel severity, began to growl. Golden sparks flashed in her eyes, as if the intense, encroaching blackness of her pupils had pushed them out of their orbits. I saw her spread her claws—they were at least as long as those of the bears in the forests. Alexander retreated a step. His eyes misted over. . .

"Forgive me," he murmured.

He was addressing both of us—it is quite unnecessary, I think, to explain that Dæmon had understood what had happened. . . I went on smiling at Alexander. Dæmon turned her head aside, perhaps out of a kind of grumpy coquetry (she adored my uncle), perhaps to make it clear that it couldn't all end as simply as that. Alexander seemed in despair. He came up to me again, bent down, and whispered in my ear:

"We can cure you ourselves. Would you like that?"

I looked at him confidently. I couldn't—or didn't want to—speak, but I nodded. He moved away, relieved, and the livid patches disfiguring his face, the rings around his tormented eyes, disappeared. He took a deep breath, and then turned to Grandmother, Grandfather, and Sonine—the latter was busy trying to console Kinga, who was wailing more desperately than ever.

"I am going to ask you to leave the room. My very dear friend" (he indicated The-Lady-In-Black) "can cure Max-Ulrich. But to do so, she needs to be alone. I—and Dæmon, of course" (he was certainly trying to conciliate her)—"will stay here to help her. Her magnetic powers must not be distracted. . ."

Everyone withdrew on tiptoe, as if the unexpected powers of the Lady radiated an atmosphere of meditation throughout the room. Sonine jibbed, but Alexander propelled her by the shoulders, requesting her to stop making her grimaces, which caused a waste of precious time. I watched everything that was going on with total tranquillity. But when the door was closed and double-locked, and my uncle crossed the room and grasped my wrists (Dæmon was still turning her back, and I could see her enormous, horn-shaped shadow on the wall), I suddenly thought: "All right, I'm going to suffer some more. . ." I sighed, and, deep down, resigned myself. I felt too weak to put up a struggle. The-Lady-In-Black, who until then had stayed in the background, entrenched behind her veils, came over to me. Dæmon must have been following her with her eyes, for when the Lady had reached my bedside, she about-faced. Dæmon was now looking warmly at me again—and I felt reassured. The-Lady-In-Black raised her veil. . .

"The main thing, Max-Ulrich, is not to be afraid."

"I'm not afraid. . ."

"Good. Turn your face over to the left a little. . ."

I did so, but I had time to see her long, thick tongue emerge from between her lips. I felt something soft, slippery, liquid, passing over the wounds Alexander had inflicted on me with his teeth. The Lady was licking me, and I had the impression that a cold, velvety reptile was slithering around at the base of my neck. . . I understood why Alexander was grasping my wrists: he was holding me above a well, which was perhaps that of death, because once again I foundered, on my bed that had turned into a frail raft; my teeth were chattering, and I was covered in icy, prickly sweat. I don't know how long the operation lasted. When I emerged, Alexander's hands had let go of my wrists. There was an itching sensation over the whole of my body, but it wasn't unpleasant. I had the feeling that life was tickling me a thousand times as a way of manifesting itself, and I snuggled down blissfully in the warm sheets, I was growing a new skin, and that too was warm. I waited until the ceiling had stopped swaying. Then I propped myself up against my pillows and said to Dæmon, who was watching over me:

"Dæmon—you too. . ."

Like The-Lady-In-Black, she extended her very rosy-red tongue, and placed it over my bites. It was hot and raspy. Far from irritating me, this rough touch made me confident that it was reinforcing the completely different touch of The-Lady-In-Black's tongue; that it was healing my wounds; obliterating them; making them forgetful. . . In my turn I tried to lick Dæmon's face, but I was still too tired. . .

"I'm cured," I murmured.

And I immediately fell asleep. A dream came to meet me, full of silky, moving tongues that licked me delightfully. But the most tender caress of all was that of my tongue playing with Dæmon's tongue. We laughed and salivated a lot.

*

I got well very quickly. I never mentioned that somber evening to Alexander. Besides, I was convinced that we were equally to blame. I shouldn't have drunk the Starka, and I shouldn't have gone and taken refuge, in the middle of a stormy night, in an attic which could only dramatize the most innocent game. Alexander must have allowed himself to be carried away by the demon of "Gra", who had turned out to be dangerous. I had no right to reproach him for his transports. We didn't play the "Game" again, and the loss of this distraction made me melancholy. Despite my extreme youth I was already thinking about bygone days, about aging: perhaps they began with one less game. I found this infinitely sadder than one more wrinkle. . .

The days passed, and Alexander announced his departure. I knew he would come back, and soon, maybe, but once again I suffered. I couldn't resign myself to these repeated deaths that partings represented. We were all unhappy, and in order to forget our sorrows we decided to put on a play, in honor of dearest Alexander. It was performed on the eve of his departure after dinner. Rows of chairs were drawn up in the salon, on which all the servants, marvellously arrayed in brightly-colored costumes, took their places. Alexander's animals (especially the white cockatoos, which were feverishly pecking at the chair legs) made an almighty din, which cheered us up a little. . . In the front row, ensconced in deep, gilded armchairs, were Grandmother, Grandfather, Alexander (extremely moved), and the guests: the Abbé Zgymunt, still pink and powdered, the inevitable Grigori, and, naturally, Countess Hedwig, who, that evening, looked like an arbor collapsing under the weight of lilacs and wisterias. . .

Without realizing it, The-Lady-In-Black and I had invented a funereal decor. Between two black-lacquered screens, on a stage hung with black velvet, we had assembled various pieces of black furniture which projected sinister shadows on to a backdrop that was also black. Silver candelabra were distributed here and there. The only thing missing in the background was a corpse. . . We had chosen a frivolous French play, curiously entitled "The Bigamous Woman." It became Slav, and we called it something like "Life and Death"—I don't remember its exact title, because we had completely transformed it. Nevertheless, I'm sure the word "Death" appeared in the programs—it couldn't have been otherwise, for Kinga had been absolutely determined to expire onstage. She had insisted on being allowed to cough, and spit blood, as she considered such manifestations to be "modern and realistic". We had a lot of trouble in getting her to admit that these pulmonary death-throes were out-of-date. However, we found a solution that would allow her to breathe her last, as she desired. . . I put out all the lights in the salon. Sonine gave the traditional French theater's three knocks, and raised the curtain (a black one, as was appropriate). The candles fluttered, and the shiny furniture slowly became visible against the dark background. Kinga was lying on a divan covered with dark, shimmering furs. She moaned, writhed in pain, and her long white hand, drooping over the side of the divan like a flower with a broken stalk, was an ominous sign of the many torments to come. We could hear a ripple of emotion among the audience. Kinga's stomach was enormously swollen, and Sonine, who was playing the part of a lady's maid, asserted:

"Madame, I tell you, I assure you, you are pregnant. . ."

Kinga refused to admit a fact that was nevertheless obvious. She claimed that she was swollen because she had eaten too much on the previous evenings, during the festivities organized in honor of the visit of a Pope of the Orthodox Church. Sonine launched into a long and rather moralistic monologue, in the course of which she inveighed against irregular lives, nightly orgies, dawns sparkling with champagne yet barbed with deadly chill. . . She went on and on about these vices, and I had to make signs to her from the wings to get her to stop her attacks on a particular set of people that I found extremely amusing. At all events, it was

112

apparent that she knew some very unexpected things. When she finally stopped, I appeared. I threw myself at Kinga's feet, for I was supposed to be one of her suitors. I expressed great sympathy for her, until the moment when I perceived her guilty curves. Then I gave way to a violent fit of rage, for I was convinced that I was not the father of her future child. Trying to calm me, Kinga began to sing, in a sweet, imploring fashion:

> *My love, my love, I have never betrayed you,*
> *My love, my love, I have always obeyed you.*
> *Pity me in my sad distress.*
> *Have faith in your loyal, true mistress.*

I replied, also singing:

> *No, I have no more faith in you,*
> *In faith, I renounce you. . . Madame, Adieu!*
> *I believed in you once, but that time is past.*
> *I love you no more; the die is cast!*

I made my exit with outraged dignity, draped in a cape a little too big for me, which caught in the door I was trying in vain to slam. Nevertheless, we were much applauded. . . Enter The-Lady-In-Black. She nourished a tragic passion for Kinga, and heaped the most terrible reproaches on her head, striding up and down the stage and drawing on her long cigarette holder. Finally, she tossed it on to the ground, stamped on it, and flung herself on to her frivolous friend's couch, intending to strangle her. Alerted by Kinga's cries, Sonine stormed in and threw herself between them:

"At least *you* are not the father," Baba shouted.

This line, which was her own invention, made some members of the audience—who were most appreciative—wild with joy. The-Lady-In-Black gave her a terrific backhander, which reverberated throughout the room because it was by no means simulated. Whereupon I rushed in, because I was still in the entrance hall (not that of the castle, but that of Kinga's private residence). My soul was in torment, but I was a man of honor. I challenged the Lady to a duel. . . At this moment, someone knocked on the door. Sonine, who had slightly recovered, went to open it. She came back in a great state of agitation and announced that a mysterious man from far-off parts was demanding to see Kinga, he had come to take care of her—but that we had to leave the room, to preserve his anonymity. We exited on tiptoe, taking some of the candelabra with us, to make the stage more crepuscular. . .

Dæmon made her entrance. The audience was spellbound. I realized this when I heard a murmur of admiration. She was more imposing than ever. She was wearing boots, and a huge felt hat with waving plumes. Naturally, hers was a silent part—but a man's part. A voice from the wings (mine) announced to the audience that Sonya (which was Kinga's name in the play) had met an exotic prince at a ball in St. Petersburg. . . They had danced waltzes and mazurkas all night long. From a palace balcony, they had watched the day dawn over the Neva. . . "And afterwards. . ."—I stopped at these ellipsis points, that spoke volumes about what might well have happened, while The-Lady-In-Black, at the piano, began to play, very softly, a polonaise. . . Dæmon walked round and round the bed, gazing at the unhappy Kinga, who murmured:

"At last. . . You have come. . . I see you, but I am dying. . . This child is yours. If he survives my death, take care of him. . . Adieu, my belovèd. . . Adieu. . . Ahhhhhhh!. . ."

Kinga sank back on to the furs. She had breathed her last. The polonaise was now barely perceptible. Dæmon froze, and then, with surprising agility, jumped on to Kinga's stomach (Kinga's whole body shuddered, but in this dramatic instant such a reaction could be attributed to one final nervous reflex). . . Dæmon sat down, her two front paws firmly joined, and in the half-light she was invested with the majesty of a sovereign statue, and her long, silky, bouffant hair seemed to evaporate into the quivering flames of the few remaining candles, which were inclining in her direction. She remained there motionless for a few seconds, her face illuminated by the candelabra of her own eyes, and then she flourished her enormous, bushy tail three times. This was the signal. I pulled on an invisible rope, which raised the side of a basket under Kinga's dress (this ingenious system had been invented by Grandfather Emeric, though he didn't know what it was destined for.) A miracle! Something like a dozen kittens emerged from the robes of the poor dead girl, and the basket disappeared into a cavity hollowed out in the divan. . . Dæmon jumped down on to the stage, while the kittens shook themselves, and then rushed down into the dumbfounded audience. The apotheosis had been accomplished, the polonaise became triumphal. I would have liked the kittens (the sons and daughters of a particularly fecund neighboring cat) to stay onstage for the final bows. But their rather lengthy promiscuity had made them nervous, and they dispersed all over the salon, where they were stroked by everyone. Naturally, we kept them all, and they showed great deference to Dæmon, who accepted them with very good grace. However, they never became very intimate. It could well be that Dæmon, who was three times as big as their mother, slightly bewildered them.

After this ultimate surprise, there were endless ovations. Sonine never stopped opening and closing the curtains, and every time Alexander disappeared from my sight I said to myself: "That's how it will be tomorrow, I shan't see him again. . ." Then he reappeared, and smiled at me, and I felt terribly sad. At one moment I thought: "I shall have to get used to it," and I imagined that the black curtain was a deep tunnel from which I had to extricate myself with all my might. But very soon I shrugged my shoulders: why these obligations, why these stupid ideas of getting used to things? I was unhappy at the present moment, what was the use of imagining a future, even a happy one? . . . Behind the curtain, now definitely closed, I burst into sobs. Dæmon rubbed herself up against me. She understood me, and I dried my tears in her warm, caressing, soothing fur—which contained the perfume of the whole of the coming winter, already surrounding us. . .

# How, Without Seeing Them, I Was Introduced into the Presence of the Celebrated Lithuanian Larvae

*T*he next day, then, at crack of dawn (as it was still dark until the morning was far advanced, it must have been about ten o'clock), Alexander kissed us all good-bye: Grandmother Casimira, Grandfather Emeric, Kinga, Sonine, and me. He promised me he would write often, that he would come back soon, that he would send more presents from Warsaw. . . Baba whimpered, and pronounced blessings on his journey. Alexander hardly needed to stoop over Dæmon, she had grown to such proportions. They embraced passionately. . . He tenderly kissed the hand of The-Lady-In-Black, and I noticed that her veil was more opaque than usual. He climbed into the barouche and installed his animals: the two leverets, the monkey in its bolero, the intolerable cockatoos, and three kittens,

117

which we had agreed to give him: Shem, Ham and Japheth. Alexander appeared at the window and put out an arm as the horses set off, and the jingling of the little bells made this livid November morning even more shivery. Soon, my uncle's hand and face were swallowed up by the snow. The barouche disappeared between the tall, rigid, tree trunks. . . We waved our handkerchiefs limply; it must have been very difficult to distinguish them from the swirling snow that had once again encroached. The only one that could be seen, fighting the snowflakes like the wing of a somber bird, was The-Lady-In-Black's black crêpe handkerchief. We went back into the castle in silence.

I felt morose. There was nothing I wanted, and Grandmother seemed to be worried about the state I was in. She came up to me and said:

"Max-Ulrich, you've been very tired, and I don't think it will do you much good to go on indefinitely watching the snow fall, behind your glasses. . . To-morrow I am going to visit my late father's estate. Why don't you come with me, you and our beloved Dæmon. . ."

I accepted with pleasure. A journey could only take my mind off things. We didn't need to make any great preparations, and the day dragged on, rather drab, rather grey, convalescent, as is always the case after a departure.

We left at the same hour as Alexander had, Grandmother Casimira, Dæmon, and I. All the time we were following the road my uncle had taken, I was immersed in somber thoughts. But we came to a crossroads and went a different way, and the sadness of the parting gradually faded: lives have to bifurcate just as quickly as roads. . . I looked at Grandmother and Dæmon, wrapped in their warm, heavy furs. I let myself be lulled into torpor by this long, muffled immersion in the white landscapes. The snow crackled, like torn silk, under the wheels of the jolting barouche. Only the horses' bells woke these dead expanses. Occasionally, when we passed a cottage, a door would half-open and a peasant woman with a shawl over her head would wave a hand. . . Or a flock of squawking birds would fly up and for a time disturb the mournful sky that was determined to snow, to snow relentlessly. . . We passed lakes trapped under the ice. We penetrated deep into forests, and the barouche brushed up against branches from which fringed and flaky feathers fell. As we were emerging from a wood, the snow intensified. It brought on a premature twilight, and we had to stop in a little town whose name I have forgotten—though not that of its hotel: "Versalis" (Versailles). In the big, cold rooms, we got ready for dinner. I put on my Warsaw clothes. Dæmon licked herself, and I brushed her for a long time, while she hummed, and her fur began to crackle, and then to glisten, revealing all the delicate nuances of her russet, brown, grey and black hairs, intricately intermingled, and distributed over her body in perfect harmony. Grandmother appeared, in a cloud of pastel-colored and only slightly faded lace. . . She had great presence.

Our entrance into the dining room attracted all eyes. I was bursting with pride in Grandmother's elegant dignity and Dæmon's irresistible grace. They gave us a table not far from an orchestra of fat, bored, badly made-up women, who wore feathers on their heads, and played hesitation-waltzes so slow and so jerky that you would have had to turn yourself into an automaton to manage to dance to them. . . And even then you would have ground to a halt, and remained in a state of suspended animation until you were wound up again with a squeaky key, to start on a new waltz. . . The wines were delicious, but the food was insipid and rather meager. We had to call several times for more vegetables and desserts for Dæmon, who was quite famished by the journey. We were just finishing our meal when one of the fat ladies wearily abandoned her enormous cello which she had been squeezing between her legs. She came up to the front of the stage, and while her colleagues began murmuring and making moaning sounds with their instruments, bowing her head as if in great torment, she sang a Prussian song about the wind. "Der Wiiiiiiiind", we heard. . . Her voice wheezed, she dragged out every syllable, and it seemed as if a glacial breeze were issuing from her throat—a dead man's last breath. Grandmother adjusted her shawl:

"This song is too chilly for me. . ."

"I quite like it," I said.

"Yes," Grandmother went on, "in the summer. . . But in the depths of winter, really. . ."

She was interrupted by a sort of ancestral figure who bowed to her very ceremoniously. He had a great mane of white hair, which made him look like a prophet. His clothes were well-cut but threadbare, outmoded, and rather grey. . .

"I have been told who you are, Madame. . . I am

120

Professor Barlewski, and I knew you when you were a child. . . Forgive this intrusion, but I could not prevent myself from coming to pay you my respects."

Grandmother looked at the strange old man through her lorgnette, and then she scrutinized the ceiling, as if she could read some answer there. . .

"Professor Barlewski. . . Professor Barlewski. . ." she repeated. "Yes, I believe I remember. You were interested in magic and the occult sciences, were you not? My father often used to speak to me of you."

"That is correct, Madame; you have an excellent memory."

"I am delighted to meet you," said Grandmother. "Do come and sit at our table. . . This is my beloved grandson Max-Ulrich, and this is my great friend the She-Cat Dæmon. . ."

I stood up and bowed; Dæmon was content to incline her head in a distinguished, rather distant fashion. . .

"You are in marvellous company," the old man murmured. "I am something of a hermit. . . How I would appreciate the presence of a charming grandson and a beautiful feline friend. . . But I must not give way to nostalgia. . . May I know what brings you to these parts?"

"I am on my way to my father's castle, to settle some business affairs. . ."

"Ah, that castle," sighed the old man, trembling.

I thought he was going to cry, because his eyelids began to blink and his eyes misted over. A little embarrassed, I turned towards the singer, who was still giving vent to her Germanic breezes.

"Yes, that castle," Grandmother went on, in a much

more assured tone of voice. "In actual fact, it worries me a little. . . I shall not enjoy plunging back, alone, into memories and decrepitude. . . Max-Ulrich and Dæmon do not know it, and it is not of their time. . . Nor do I wish to sadden them with the thought of change and decay. . . Why should you not accompany us?"

The professor seemed surprised, then moved, and agitated. . .

"Accompany you?" he asked, wringing his hands until their joints cracked. . . "But that would give me immense pleasure. . . I was only passing through this district, but I shall be delighted to attend you. . ."

And so we left the little town, and the hotel, in the company of Professor Barlewski, after a glacial night during which I implored Dæmon to smother me, I was so cold in that Versailles among the blizzards. . .

And we continued on the long, glistening road. Animals watched us, a little blurred behind the snowflakes. Some returned to their coverts, terrified by this barouche transporting doughty travellers. The professor had fallen asleep, and was emitting a gentle wheezing sound. Grandmother was trying to read poetry, but the letters were bobbing up and down, and the lines she recited to me didn't make the slightest sense. Dæmon was observing the passing stars sticking to the windowpanes. They were perpetually changing their shapes, transforming themselves, swirling around as if in a wintry kaleidoscope. . . But snow makes you drowsy. She kept yawning. So did I.

At last we entered the castle park. Under its blanket

of snow, it was no different from the surrounding countryside. It was only the huge trees, even though they were all bare except for the conifers, that seemed more majestic. I was surprised to catch a glimpse of Chinese bridges, a pagoda, bandstands, crumbling columns, a little minaret, and an infinite number of mutilated statues, which the cold made even more immobile. One of them had lost its arms, an⁚ I thought of those unfortunate people who have to have limbs amputated because they have been exposed too long to the ice. . .

Grandmother told me that her father was fond of geographical diversions. Fancy-dress balls were organized near the minaret; torch-lit concerts in the pagoda; plays, in peplums, in front of the colonnades. . .

"Were those 'the good old days'?" I asked.

"No," Grandmother replied, "they were quite simply 'bygone days'."

Professor Barlewski had adopted an ecstatic air—I couldn't understand why. Perhaps because, unlike Grandmother, for him bygone days did represent the good old days. . .

The castle was rather similar to ours. It was built of red brick, in the usual neo-gothic style. It had two storeys and four angle towers. We were received upstairs, because the ground floor rooms were damp and no longer in use. Not that the ones above were much better (I saw nothing but torn hangings, ill-assorted and rickety furniture), but there were great fires blazing in the hearths. They warmed and comforted us, as did the abundant meal we were served. When we had finished it, Grandmother had to attend to her business. She took Professor Barlewski into a sinister office, where farmers and bailiffs were awaiting her. . . I was left alone with Dæmon, who was digesting her meal in front of the flames. I went over to one of the windows and contemplated the park. In such weather the whole countryside was deserted, but it seemed to me to be worse than abandoned: forgotten, lost, aslant, adrift. I was preoccupied with those "bygone days" Grandmother had spoken about. I thought it would take our minds off things if Dæmon and I went for a walk. I laced up her boots, I put mine on, and, enveloped in our capes, we crunched through the crisp snow. I was especially attracted by the pagoda. With some difficulty, we made our way up the little hill on which it was situated. When we had reached it, I heard whistling sounds, which echoed and re-echoed. . . I pushed the door open, and we found ourselves in an empty, cylindrical room, exposed to all the winds. The snow was seeping through the cracked, disintegrating walls, and had become a kind of temporary mortar holding up the fragile framework of the elaborate, rotting, Chinese panels. In this rotunda, as I contemplated those myriads of glittering crevices, I had the impression that I was in the center of a cyclorama representing the sparkling, dusty, Milky Way. Dæmon and I began to spin around like whirling dervishes, faster and faster, and those thousands of flickering lights went flashing past our eyes like shooting stars; they spattered us with frozen silver, we plunged into the very heart of the fireworks, their rockets were made of frost, they intoxicated us, bemused us. . . At one moment, against that shimmering background which was like gleaming water, I caught a glimpse of Dæmon's deep gold eyes. I saw in a flash the contrast between their fire and the encircling ice; the landscapes became telescoped. . . I was perfectly willing to admit that this pagoda was capable of skating over the snows of Lithuania. . . I suddenly decided that I had been born nowhere; that it was good to live like that, without restrictions, without frontiers, without a "fatherland", at the mercy of the whims of journeys and of the weather. The weather! . . . It was becoming terrible. Just like a fever, the wind and snow increased tenfold with the approach of twilight. We were caught in a flurry, maybe even in a snowstorm. . . We staggered out, blinded by the snowflakes which by evening had had time to acquire a cutting edge, and they slashed our faces like razor-blades. We rushed down the hill as quickly as we could. As we reached the bottom, we heard a strange, muffled, almost discreet noise. We turned, and saw the roof of the pagoda swaying, leaning over to one side like a crooked conical hat, and then slipping, while the walls of the fragile edifice slowly collapsed into the snow. The pagoda had disappeared! We raced up the castle steps. Grandmother had finished her negotiations. Panting, I shouted to her:

"Grandmother, Grandmother, the pagoda doesn't exist anymore, it's collapsed. . ."

Grandmother looked at me in surprise. She smiled, and took me in her arms:

"Max-Ulrich, you mustn't let yourself get into such a state. Never mind about the pagoda. . . I can't keep

125

this estate up anymore, and I have sold it. . . I'm sorry about the charming pagoda. . . Like you, I loved it. . . But it did well to disappear. . . What it really stood for was a unique nostalgia. Instead of thinking about all that I am abandoning, tomorrow I shall think that the pagoda is the only thing I am leaving behind me, here. The parting will be a wrench, but less materialistic. Poor pagoda, poor concerts, poor home. . ." Her voice trembled. She seemed dreamy, moved. . . "We shall ask Grandfather to have one built at the castle, in place of the cannons. . ." She took hold of herself. "And now, let us go and have dinner, we have great need of it. . ."

We were presented with a succession of solid, copious dishes, to which we did justice. The professor threw himself on the food as if he hadn't eaten for several days. He got bits of it all over his collar, and kept slobbering. After this rustic feast which, strangely enough, in no way displeased Dæmon (she even consented to lap up the brown, unctuous sauces of the gamey meat), we sat down in the unmatched armchairs in front of the tall fireplace. I felt blissfully happy. Dæmon was breathing heavily. Grandmother was pretending to listen to Professor Barlewski—but it was only the circles of her lorgnette that were wide-eyed. Behind the lenses, her eyelids kept dropping. . . Fortunately, the professor was a loquacious and absentminded sort of man, and he never stopped talking about the fin de siècle Polish poets he had known and admired. He had just begun to speak of Strindberg, when I noticed that he was fidgeting nervously. I watched his movements, and decided that they must be due to his uncomfortable position. Following the example of Grandmother and Dæmon, I had let myself drift into a state of pleasant, warm somnolence when the professor suddenly jumped, and uttered a shrill cry. He must have woken Grandmother, for she said:

"My dear friend, you must be sitting on a broken spring. . . Try another armchair. . ."

"No, it isn't that. . . I feel as if I have been stung. . . it's terrible, it's frightful. . ."

Perhaps Professor Barlewski was suffering from a painful skin disease, but we were either too lazy or too polite to dare to question him about what was making him itch. Nevertheless, we were surprised when he flew into a rage and started yelling:

"To hell with poetry, to hell with Strindberg. . ."

He half sat up on his seat and started furiously flicking at his hands and at his face, which was pale with fury under his dishevelled white hair. Grandmother couldn't stand it any longer. She waved her lorgnette, and demanded:

"But Professor, whatever is the matter?"

He didn't say a word, and he didn't even look at her. He suddenly leaped up, his eyes staring, his nostrils dilated, and started running in circles around the armchairs. I thought we must be in the presence of a lunatic, and I settled back comfortably in my chair, imitated, I may add, by Dæmon, the better to appreciate his antics. Distractions were rare in Lithuania. . . I didn't for a moment think he might be dangerous—but he certainly was surprising. . . Not content with scouring every portion of the salon, he knelt down at each corner, lowered his head, shook it, and sniffed noisily. . .

"Hmm, Hmm, Hmm," we heard.

Grandmother Casimira, Dæmon and I exchanged looks. It was Grandmother who broke our silent stupor. . .

"Really, Professor, you worry us. . ." she articulated, in a tense voice.

The professor shook his locks, looked at her in obvious despair, and exclaimed:

"With good reason, Madame, and we are in grave danger."

"In danger?" I cried excitedly. "But why?"

"Because we are imprisoned in the snows, and we shall have to spend the night here."

"For goodness' sake say what you mean," Grandmother commanded him, exasperated. . .

Still on his knees, the professor sighed:

"Madame, are there ponds in this neighborhood?"

"Of course there are, an infinite number of beautiful grey ponds. . ."

"And marshes too, no doubt?"

"Yes, a great many marshes, and some of them are extremely disquieting. . ."

"I suppose that, in the mornings, the countryside is shrouded in mist? . . ."

"Naturally. And it is extremely poetic. . ."

The professor brightened. He began to tremble—it was obvious that he was jubilant.

"That's it, that's it," he exclaimed. "And you have never noticed anything?"

Grandmother pretended to be reflecting:

"No. . . Well, as you know, I only lived here for short periods, during my childhood. . . Later, I came only occasionally, to deal with business matters, as

Emeric hates such activities. And now, I am about to leave this estate for ever. . ."

"You are well advised to do so, Madame," said the professor, in solemn, ponderous tones. . . "I have to inform you that the park, the environs, the castle, and even this room in which we find ourselves, are infested with Larvae!"

"With Larvae?" Grandmother cried.

"With Larvae?" I echoed.

Dæmon sat up in her armchair and began to examine her fur, as if it concealed some treacherous, abominable creatures. The professor stretched out his hands.

"Precisely. . . Larvae. . . I am covered in them, and I shall have the greatest difficulty in ridding myself of them."

"But what are they like?" I asked, very anxious to improve my mind.

"Like this," the professor shouted. . .

He came up to us, stood very still and very straight, screwed up his eyes and hollowed his pale, wizened cheeks, thus imposing a bizarre process of suction on his thin lips. In my eyes, the professor had been transformed into The-Great-Lithuanian-Larva, and I shall never forget this quasi-magical metamorphosis. . . Grandmother brought a hand up to her bosom:

"But Professor: these Larvae, as you call them . . . Are they dangerous?"

"Not too dangerous," replied the professor, "as we shall only be spending one night here. . . But they can be debilitating, very debilitating. . ."

"Is there anything we can do?"

Grandmother was becoming worried. . .

"I think so. . . Later, when I am alone in my room, I shall give myself a little first aid treatment, for, Thank God, I never travel without unguents. . . But what you need, dearest friend, for your protection, and for that of your grandson and your dear Dæmon, is milk, some good, fresh milk, in bowls distributed around your beds. . . And now I must leave you. . . Please excuse me. . ."

The professor had once again begun to scratch himself furiously, and he went galloping out of the room.

We asked the servants to surround our beds with receptacles filled to the brim with very fresh milk. They looked at us in amazement, as if they hadn't quite understood, and then did as they were asked, shaking their heads. After all, we came from elsewhere. We might well have strange whims. . .

When we kissed Grandmother goodnight, she told us we weren't to worry. But I guessed that she had more misgivings than Dæmon or I. Nevertheless, I bolted the door to my room. With some difficulty I climbed up into the very high bed. Dæmon joined me very nimbly. I stroked her, watching the snowflakes fall, because I had forgotten to draw the curtains. I thought about Professor-Larva, and about the Lithuanian-Larvae that were no doubt lying in wait for us. . . I wondered whether I ought to be frightened, just a little bit frightened. From my bed, I contemplated the bowls of milk surrounding me. I thought about the ruined pagoda, about this castle which Grandmother would never see again. . . I imagined that a great snowstorm had swept through it and left evenly-spaced, round white patches on the floor, which glistened in the darkness like little iced-up puddles. Dæmon was already asleep—I followed her example, holding one of her paws, with her soft fur tickling my nose. . .

When I awoke the next morning, I saw that the ice had melted. . . No—that the Larvae, the gluttons, had drunk all the milk. Barefoot and in my nightshirt, I ran to Grandmother's room. I beat a tattoo on her door, because she too had locked herself in. . . When she opened the door I was flabbergasted: the bowls around her bed were still full! Alerted by my cries, the professor came hurrying up. He and Grandmother followed me into my room. When he saw the empty receptacles he was overjoyed—although he was still scratching himself.

"This child has had a narrow escape. . . God be praised, I saved him from those pernicious creatures. . ."

Then I noticed Dæmon. She was licking her chops, before starting on her morning toilet. I ran over to her, because in my agitation I had forgotten to wish her good morning. I put my arms around her and kissed her passionately. I realized that, in just one night, she had grown even bigger and fatter. When would she ever stop? But why impose limits. . . ? As her size increased, so did my love for her. "Dæmon. . . , Dæmon. . ." I murmured her name, delivered from my fear of the vigilant Larvae, and convinced that she had protected me, for Larvae must be horribly afraid of Great-Exceptional-She-Cats. She licked me affectionately—and took not the slightest interest in the empty milk bowls. She seemed angelic and carefree—

131

but when she turned around, I noticed that she was belching a lot. . .

*

We left Professor Barlewski, whose hands and face were terribly scratched, in the town where the "Versalis" hotel was. Grandmother asked me whether I would like to spend the night there.

"No. . . No. . . ," I replied, "Let's go straight home. . ."

So we went on our way, after saying goodbye to the poor professor. It was snowing less, and the barouche was going at a good speed. . . With each jolt, Dæmon gave a great hiccup. She refused all food when we stopped for lunch and dinner. Gradually night fell all around us, although the snow made it seem less dark, and more than once I mistook a stray snowflake for a shooting star. Soon we entered a forest in which eyes were shining. I knew that Grandmother had a bag full of money on her knees.

"Do you think we're going to be attacked by brigands?" I asked her.

She burst out laughing. . .

"I don't think so."

I laughed too. Larvae. . . Bandits. . . I mustn't expect too much. As the gentle, pendulum-like movement of the swaying barouche registered the passing of the hours, and as we approached the castle, I began to feel full of joy. In the first place, there was the pleasure of waking the whole household in the middle of the night, and then there were a thousand things to relate, to exaggerate: the ladies' orchestra, the dinner, the appearance of Professor Barlewski, the loss of the

132

castle, the collapse of the pagoda, the attack of the Larvae—all this in one evening and one day. I thought up some phrases, and a few tiny white lies, and then, between the long, intertwined fingers of the bare branches, I saw a light. . .

"The castle," I murmured.

I breathed a sigh of satisfaction. In a few minutes I would see Kinga, Sonine, The-Lady-In-Black, Grandfather Emeric. . . A wave of happiness, of warmth swept over me. We had just come through the ever-open gate, and as we drove on, glimmers of light appeared in the windows. Quite soon we stopped by the portico. Grandfather was standing on the steps. He stretched out his arms. . .

"We were beginning to feel worried. . ." he said, with relief in his voice.

Hardly had she set paw on the snow, than Dæmon began to vomit a whitish liquid. We were very worried, but she accepted the light midnight meal prepared for us with very good grace. We concluded that her brief malaise had been caused by the movements of the barouche. Everyone fussed around us, and I found it delightful to be questioned and embraced by people in their nightclothes. I had crossed many "niorsts" (kilometers) of infinite white expanses. . . I had come from "out there", from the night. . . The castle had come to meet us, over the snow, to shelter us, and I was going to fall asleep with Dæmon, in our room—after a long journey that had lasted three days. . .

# . . . The Winter—
# The Long, Beautiful,
# Eternal Winter. . .

*A*nd the snowflakes continued to blur what we could glimpse of the countryside. And the layers of snow became thicker and thicker. Winter had arrived—as we learned from a date on the calendar, because for the rest, nothing changed. Grandfather Emeric occupied himself with his collections. Grandmother Casimira embroidered or read. Sonine was very busy preparing the Christmas and New Year festivities. The-Lady-In-Black taught Kinga and me whatever we wanted to learn. I had letters from my Uncle Alexander—he would be coming for Christmas. . .

The Winter continued, and yet everything seemed to be in a state of torpor, because of the silence, the isolation, the peace. . . And I want to take advantage of the immobility of that snowbound castle and cheat a little—mix up the days and the strata of my memories and no longer turn back to the past, but speak in the present tense. . . I need to go quickly, it's all so close to my heart.

Yes, Winter is here, the long, the very long Winter, and today Dæmon and I are going for a walk in the grounds because the pale sky, which seems to reflect all the neighboring ponds, has lost its clouds. Dæmon has grown to the almost unimaginable size of a big Saint Bernard, and the rather primitive peasants hang offerings for her on what remains of the park gates. . .

She sometimes goes out without me. With a resolute step she plunges into the deep snow. I watch her from one of the castle windows until she disappears from my sight. And then I curse my myopia, and the torments that cruelly hide her from me. Where does she go? I shall never know.

We often go for a sleigh ride, muffled up to our ears in thick furs. Snowflakes sting our faces, cling to my eyelashes and to Dæmon's vast, delicate vibrissae, which quiver and sparkle like silver threads. As we fly through the wind, it robs her of this previous metal, but her enormous, golden, copper-veined eyes, with their two black stars, remain wide open and staring. The horses' bells jingle merrily, like ice-cubes tinkling in a glass, the landscapes accelerate, we snuggle up together and keep each other warm. We are going so far. . .

We sometimes go skating on a little frozen lake. Dæmon strikes out, and glides along on the smooth,

135

taut little cushions under her paws. When she wants to stop, she spreads her claws. Thanks to them she can describe some very lovely sinusoidal curves which my skates would be totally incapable of making. . . I take Uncle Alexander's gramophone, and we can waltz, we can go off in opposite directions and then come back to each other, while the alder trees on the banks of the lake bow their heads, and our own heads spin.

I don't like it when Dæmon vanishes into the twilight. There have been dreadful rumors—children have disappeared. I don't really think she eats them, but a blue silk ribbon was found on the snow, and, farther off, a little, roughly-carved wooden toy. But in any case—and I am quite sure of this—she doesn't attack animals. . .

I must admit that it's the nights I like best. I'm never cold anymore. I don't need the blazing fires in the hearths, or the faïence stoves, or the potbellied eiderdowns. I snatch off my shirt and lie down on my bed, naked. Slowly, Dæmon comes up to me and covers me with all her warm fur. I lose myself in her long, long hairs—and yet I don't suffocate, she doesn't suffocate me. I hold my breath. I stare at her. She stares at me; maybe she even hypnotizes me. I would so like to stay awake. But I bury myself in her gaze, I murmur her name, I feel her voluptuous softness, a great dark cope envelops us, the bed floats in the darkness; outside, the snow is falling; here, our caresses are in harmony. . .

. . . Here, in Lithuania, in this wintry, nocturnal castle, where Dæmon sleeps and dreams—and where I dream of her, Dæmon, in Lithuania. . .

136